"You're too close to the windows," Cole said softly as if he understood everything going through her mind and didn't want to intrude, but needed to keep her safe.

Alyssa looked up at him and for the first time she really understood the law enforcement mentality. Police officers were strong protectors and they always wanted to be ready to help. Even being married to an officer for seven years, she hadn't really felt the weight of the burden they bore until this dangerous situation invaded her life.

She glanced at the black wall of windows Cole had warned her away from. "Guess you're wishing you'd rented a house with fewer windows."

"I have to admit it would be easier," he said with steel in his voice. "But I'm not going to let these windows stop me. I'll do everything within my power to protect you, even if it means giving up my life."

She knew he spoke the truth and she feared before all of this was over, he would have to choose between protecting her and putting his life on the line.

Books by Susan Sleeman

Love Inspired Suspense

High-Stakes Inheritance
Behind the Badge
The Christmas Witness
*Double Exposure
*Dead Wrong
*No Way Out

*The Justice Agency

SUSAN SLEEMAN

grew up in a small Wisconsin town where she spent her summers reading Nancy Drew and developing a love of mystery and suspense books. Today she channels this enthusiasm into hosting the popular internet website *TheSuspenseZone.com* and writing romantic-suspense and mystery novels.

Much to her husband's chagrin, Susan loves to look at everyday situations and turn them into murder-and-mayhem scenarios for future novels. If you've met Susan, she has probably figured out a plausible way to kill you and get away with it.

Susan currently lives in Florida, but has had the pleasure of living in nine states. Her husband is a church music director and they have two beautiful daughters, a very special son-in-law and an adorable grandson. To learn more about Susan, please visit www.SusanSleeman.com.

No Way Out

Susan Sleeman

HARLEQUIN LOVE INSPIRED SUSPENSE

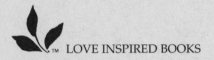

LOVE INSPIRED BOOKS

ISBN-13: 978-0-373-18572-6

NO WAY OUT

www.LoveInspiredBooks.com

Printed in U.S.A.

You will keep in perfect peace those whose minds
are steadfast, because they trust in you.
—*Isaiah* 26:3

For my sister and brother, Linda and Jeff Becker,
the siblings in my life who inspired me to
write about the dynamics of the Justice family.

Additional thanks to

My family: my husband, Mark,
who willingly makes sacrifices so I can devote
my time to writing; my daughter Emma
who helps me work through plot issues
and Erin for her graphic design expertise.

My patient, sweet and talented editor, Tina James.
Thank you for continuing to have faith
in my writing.

The very generous Ron Norris—
retired police officer with the
LaVerne Police Department—who gives of
his time and knowledge in both police procedures
as well as military information. Thank you
for always answering my questions so thoroughly
and so promptly. You go above and beyond,
and I can't thank you enough! Any errors in or
liberties taken with the technical details Ron
so patiently explained to me are all my doing.

And most importantly, thank you God
for my faith and for giving me daily challenges
to grow closer to you.

ONE

A storm was coming.

Alyssa Wells slowed and glanced across the road at waves angrily pounding the deserted Oregon beach. A sudden movement on the jogging path below caught her attention. Nearly finished with her run, she looked down at a clearing where hikers often stopped to gaze over the ocean.

But not at this time of night. Not with ominous clouds building over the horizon.

Angry voices swirled out of the soupy fog that had rolled in with the setting sun. The harsh words cut through the night and wound their way up the hill. She stopped in surprise when she recognized one of the voices as that of Nolan Saunders, her neighbor and her deceased husband's partner on the Pacific Bay police force.

What was Nolan doing out here with a storm on its way?

She recalled that he was on duty tonight—he must have responded to a call here. No matter—she needed to get home to her twins before the clouds burst. She continued ahead on the trail, grateful for tiny solar lights mounted on wooden landscape beams that cast a dull light over her feet and kept her path unobscured.

"You're in too deep to walk away, Gibson." Nolan's raised voice, now sharp and clear, sent a whisper of unease down her back, and she came to a stop directly above them. She could make out the shadows of three men. The "Gibson" Nolan talked to must be fellow officer Frank Gibson, but who was the third guy?

"C'mon, Saunders, I have to get out," Frank said, sounding desperate.

Nolan stepped closer, and Alyssa saw him stab his finger into Frank's chest. "That's not gonna happen, pal. Once a meth dealer, always a meth dealer."

Meth? Her husband, Todd, had died on the job from a fatal gunshot to the chest, but the resulting investigation found meth in his blood. They also linked him to a meth distribution ring, and he'd been branded a dirty cop.

Had Todd worked with Nolan and Frank to distribute drugs? Was the whole Pacific Bay police force dirty?

"You came to me, remember?" Nolan continued. "Said you needed the money."

"That's because Danny was sick." Alyssa had been praying for Frank's son in his battle with leukemia. "Now that he's in remission we're caught up on our bills and I want out."

"See, here's the problem." Nolan moved closer to Frank. "There was no time limit on our association. You said you were with us for the long haul. Now a few of our dealers are busted and you want to run home to mama. Too bad. You belong to me now."

"Just let me walk away, man," Frank pleaded. "I don't want to go to jail, but I can't live with the guilt anymore. I'll turn you in if that's my only way out."

"What makes you think I'll let you rat us out?" Nolan's volume had dropped, but it held twice the threat. "There're other options if you decide to bail."

"Like what?" Frank paused, and she could imagine him glaring at Nolan. "Fine. You're too chicken to say it so I will. I'll end up a homicide statistic and framed as a drug dealer just like Todd."

"Just like Todd. Dead and buried," Nolan answered. "But in your case there won't be a need to frame you."

Oh my goodness, Todd!

Nolan said "framed." Maybe her husband hadn't been dirty. Maybe he'd found out about the meth operation and threatened to report Nolan. Then Nolan had killed Todd and framed him.

Nausea rose up her throat followed by a rush of anger. She considered Nolan a friend. He'd been there for her since Todd was murdered. Had let her and her seven-year-old twins live in one side of his duplex rent free. Helped her care for the children, becoming like a brother to her and an uncle to them.

She wanted to climb down the hill and confront him. She took a step.

No. She couldn't. If what Nolan said was

true, he was dangerous. A murderer! She had to get out of here before he discovered her. Once she was away from him, she could take her time to figure out what to do.

The men continued to argue as she set off slowly for fear of making any noise. She made it a few feet when a blustery wind pummeled her body, knocking her off balance. She tried to right herself, but her foot caught on a rock, and she tumbled onto her hands and knees, smacking into the path with an audible thud.

"Someone's here," Nolan said in that deadly-calm voice. "On the upper path."

"You think they heard us?" the third man asked.

"I don't know, but we're not taking any chances," Nolan said. "Get 'em."

Barely able to see through the thickening fog, Alyssa pushed to her feet. With the tiny landscape lights as her only guide, she ran. Hard and fast. Each step sent her heart beating faster. Powerful winds threatened to take her down, but she kept her footing and continued.

She heard heavy footfalls pounding on the path below her. They were heading in the same direction—toward the downtown parking lot holding her car. They were a bit behind her, but Nolan's long legs would catch her in no time.

She picked up speed. Sharp pellets of rain assaulted her face, soaking her lightweight running jacket and weighing her down.

The storm was upon them. Full force now. Raging and angry. She was struggling to get through the wind gusts and driving rain but took comfort from the knowledge that they would be struggling, too.

She heard footfalls growing closer. *Thud, thud, thud*—they pounded on the soft soil that sucked at her feet. She fought hard to stay on course for the main road.

No. Don't go there. That's where they'd have parked their cars.

She had to think defensively. It would be too easy for them to catch her on the open road.

She took a leap and plunged into the ditch ahead of them. She slogged through waist high grass, the sharp blades slicing into her hands. She raised them high.

"He's in the ditch. Get him," Nolan called out to his buddies.

Good, he thought she was a man, which meant her identity was safe. *If* she managed to outrun them.

She kept going, her side hitching and her body begging to stop. Her pace faltered, and she slowed. The faces of her precious twins flashed in her mind. She had to make it out of here for them. She moaned with pain but pumped her legs harder. Her muscles burned but the ground disappeared behind her and the sound of her assailants finally fell off.

Stopping, she filled her lungs with air and listened.

Silence. Nothing but blessed silence, save the howling wind and brutal rain.

They wouldn't have given up. They'd probably gone to get their cars.

If she kept going while they backtracked, she had a chance to escape before they figured out her identity. But where should she go?

She searched the area. The beach.

Yes, that's it.

They couldn't follow her there in their cars.

Lungs still screaming for air, she kicked into gear again. When she saw no traffic, she crossed the road, barreling down the hill and onto the sand. She heard sirens swirling closer and then stopping on the road behind her.

No! They must have seen the direction she'd headed. She was too far away for them to identify her for now, but they would soon be tracking her on foot again. Her worst nightmare was coming true. They'd catch her and her children would be orphans.

She wouldn't let that happen. She raced toward the icy water and paralleled the shore, letting pounding waves erase her footprints. She hoped by the time they parked their car and made it down to the water that she'd be far enough away and they wouldn't be able to see the direction she'd run.

Cold sliced up her legs and tightened her muscles. She wanted to crumple onto the sand, but her only hope was to take shelter in her favorite spot. She often took her morning run along the softly flowing tides then sat on an outcropping of rocks and watched the waves, wishing for things that could never be.

Things she thought she'd attain by the time she turned thirty-two but had remained elusive in her life.

Tonight, instead of wishing, she could rest there and make a plan. Very few people knew about her spot, and she would be safe.

She heard raised male voices behind her, and she wrenched around to look. She couldn't see the men yet but feared they'd found her.

"Father, please let me make it. For the children." Her words evaporated in the swirling storm that was picking up in intensity.

She had to reach the rocks. Just had to, before they tracked her down and fired a bullet in her heart as they'd done to Todd.

Cole Justice pushed away hair plastered against his forehead and looked over the pounding surf. A big storm was on its way in from the Pacific, and he'd climbed a large boulder—the highest point on the beach— to watch. Foolhardy move, he was sure. The rocks were slippery and the night dark, but he liked it best in the dark these days. Away from the concerned stares of his family. Away from the constant self-recriminations.

As he stared at the angry sea, the clouds parted and the moon highlighted the beach. He saw someone moving in the hazy mist. Odd. He'd figured he was the only one foolish enough to brave the spitting rain in a winter storm on the Oregon coast.

The tall figure raced along the water's edge, glancing back every so often as if someone was in pursuit. The "danger" instincts, honed during his second tour of duty in Iraq, sprang into full alert and he felt apprehensive, as if a threat waited in the wings to take him down.

He tried to squelch it, but there it was, burning in his gut. He'd been home for two years now and it still lingered.

Always on alert. Always watchful. Always uneasy.

He checked to make sure his weapon was still tucked in the back of his jeans and ready if he needed it. Even if he wasn't a private investigator, he was a former deputy marshal and like most former law enforcement officers, he carried all the time. Right now, he was glad he did. Something wasn't right about the figure moving closer.

Long, lithe, agile. A woman? Out here tonight?

He lifted his hand against the driving rain and stared. Yeah, it was a woman. She raced toward him with graceful strides, but he lost sight of her at the base of his rocky fortress jutting into the water. Though he didn't have a visual on her, his sniper training taught him to be still and pay attention. The sixth sense warned him that she was climbing up the face toward him.

Man, was she in for a surprise when she found him up here.

Question was, when did he let her know of his presence? If he called out to her now she could lose her focus and fall. If he waited until she got to the top and she startled backward, the fall would be fatal.

Her head popped over the rock and even in the rain, he could see her concentration. He needed to wait before saying anything.

She pulled up and fell on her stomach, dragging in huge gulps of air.

"Not a good night for a run," he said as

calmly as he could, bracing his legs against the rocks should she decide to attack and dislodge him from his perch.

She rolled and came to her knees, her arms outstretched in a defensive posture.

"Relax," he added. "I'm not here to hurt you."

She didn't move. Didn't speak.

"You can trust me," he said from his position on the ledge. "I'm not here to hurt you. I'm renting a house up the beach, and I came out to watch the storm."

She still didn't back away, but she glanced to her right before flattening herself on the rock again. He looked down the beach in the direction she'd checked and spotted two bulky figures heading their way. She *was* being chased. And now she'd put him in danger, too.

He slowly eased to his knees, keeping his head low and sliding onto the rock next to her. She turned her head and locked eyes with him.

"What're you doing?" she hissed.

"I was a sitting duck on that ledge," he whispered back. With no more than twelve inches between them, he could finally get a good look at her face. Fine boned. High cheeks and forehead. Went well with the lithe figure he saw running. And despite her mad dash down the beach, a hint of her sweet perfume lingered. So sweet he almost forgot that two men were coming after her. Almost.

"Care to fill me in on what's going on here?" he asked.

She lay motionless for a moment before she took in a deep breath. "No time. The men after me are killers."

"Are they trying to kill you?"

"Maybe. I'm not sure." She sounded so sad that it broke his heart. Something he didn't think it was capable of doing anymore. "I overheard them talking about illegal activities they're involved in. Now I think they want to kill me so I can't tell anyone what I heard."

Male voices mixed with the wind. They were coming closer. He held his finger to his lips but took the time to search her face for any duplicity. All he saw besides large eyes ringed with long lashes was fear. Raw and fresh. Even if she wasn't telling him the truth about what had happened, it was clear she was afraid of these men.

"I don't see anyone, Gibson," a deep voice rumbled from below. "We don't even know if the person came down to the beach. It's freaking cold out here, and we should call it quits."

"Quit being such a baby." The second man's voice was higher, more nasal.

The woman started shivering, and her lips quivered. Cole wore a slicker over a thick parka, but her lightweight jacket was plastered against her body. He wanted to draw her against him for warmth, but he couldn't risk her decking him and signaling their location to the men below.

"Maybe Saunders was wrong and no one heard us."

"You want to be the one to tell him that?" That high voice went even higher.

The other guy snorted. "Not if I want to live."

"That's what I figured. C'mon. We'll keep going. If we don't find someone in thirty minutes we'll quit."

Cole would give the men time to move out

of hearing distance and then he'd ask her for details to see how he could be of assistance.

She started moving as if she intended to climb over him and down to the beach.

"Not yet." Cole laid a restraining hand on her back. "We'll wait until they've put some distance between us."

"We?" Her forehead furrowed and her whole body shook from the cold.

"You need help, and I can provide it."

"I don't even know you." It took a strong woman to be this chilled and tired and refuse help. Or a foolish one.

"Then let's remedy that." He turned on his side and offered his hand. "Cole Justice. Former U.S. Marshal and Oregon National Guard," he said, hoping she'd realize he was one of the good guys.

She looked at him as if he'd lost his mind.

"Usually this is when you shake hands and give me your name." He smiled to try to ease her obvious concern, but it didn't work. She kept peering at him. "Okay. So you don't want me to know who you are. Can you at least give me a first name?"

"Alyssa," she said between tremors.

A perfectly elegant name for a woman who he figured would live up to it, if she was dry and not lying on a slimy rock with the winds and rain from the Pacific Ocean pummeling her body.

"Do you have somewhere safe to go?" he asked.

"No."

"We can go to my house until you figure out what to do."

"Not hardly."

"Look, I'm the last guy who'd tell a woman to go home with a strange man, but I really am one of the good guys. Plus my sister is staying with me so we won't be alone." He could see she was starting to consider it. "You can dry off and warm up then leave as soon as you have a plan."

"I'm all for getting off the beach until these guys take off, but I'm not stepping inside the door until I see this sister." He loved the timbre of her voice, strong and determined as if nothing could best her.

"Deal," he said. "Let me make sure they've moved far enough up the beach, then we can leave." He slid on his belly across the rock and, before glancing over the edge, he put his hand on his gun in case he needed to draw. The men were mere shadows moving away from them. He looked back at Alyssa and pushed up to his knees. "Are you good to get down on your own?"

She sat up and nodded, but she was shivering violently now. He slipped out of his slicker and parka and handed them to her. "These should help."

"No, they're yours."

"Take them," he insisted and dropped them into her hands.

She reluctantly slipped into jackets twice her size and clutched the excess fabric around her waist.

"I'll go first to be sure we're still alone." He didn't wait for her agreement but lowered his body over the edge and descended as quickly as he could without endangering his life.

She was on her way down before he hit the ground. Hand on his weapon, he quickly checked the other side of the rock to be sure they were alone. He wanted to draw his gun, but he figured Alyssa would run from him if she knew he was armed. Most people didn't understand that it was normal for law enforcement officers, even former or retired officers, to carry all the time.

He cleared the side of the rock and a gust of wind hit him full on, soaking him anew. The storm was picking up. They had to get a move on. He ran back to the rocks and waited for Alyssa. About five feet above him, she missed a foothold and fell backward. No scream, no flailing, just a soft free-fall into his arms that strained with his catch.

Her eyes were wide open with the same fear in the depths but still in control. She was the coolest woman he'd ever met. As if nothing fazed her.

"Thank you," she said and pushed out of his hold. "We should go."

The wind howled around the rock, spitting seawater and sand. When they stepped into the open she'd have a hard time without support, but he'd wait for her to ask for his help.

"This way." He started up the beach, the wet sand packing nicely under his feet and making the going easier. He kept looking back to check on her. She was falling behind. He slowed to let her catch up. "We'd make better time if you'd hold on to me to keep the wind from carrying you off course."

She studied him a moment then gave a clipped nod and cautiously approached him. He lifted his arm and she slipped under it. *A perfect fit,* he couldn't help but think.

She was still shivering so he pulled her tighter against his body. She wrapped an arm around his waist and they trudged up the beach.

As the wind blew harder, he could feel her faltering. He looked down at her, and she seemed fragile and small. It touched him in a place he thought long dead from the ravages of war. He bent and scooped her into his arms. Her mouth formed an O of surprise, but she didn't protest so he set off again, her head against chest, his head bent against the wind. He climbed the wooden stairs to his deck overlooking the beach and crossed to the door.

"Your sister," she said pointedly, strength still in her voice even if it had left her body.

He smiled at her tenacity and pounded on the door.

"You can put me down now," she said.

"You'll stay warmer this way." Surprisingly she didn't struggle but rested her head on his chest again. He figured she really had to be wiped out to do so.

The door opened and, though his sister Dani's mouth dropped open in surprise at the sight of them, she didn't ask any questions. Not that Cole routinely brought home women in distress, but their family did run a private investigation agency dedicated to helping people who had nowhere else to turn. She was used to seeing people in need.

"Alyssa, meet Dani." He turned his attention back to Alyssa. "Can we go in now?"

When her lips tipped in a charming smile, he had to draw in a breath at the stunning beauty.

"Get some blankets, Dani." He crossed the threshold and headed for the sofa. "And lock the door."

Dani turned the dead bolt then ran down the hallway. She returned with blankets as Cole gently set Alyssa on the sofa. Dani shook out a blanket and wrapped it around Alyssa's shaking shoulders.

"Thank you." Alyssa smiled again, her lips trembling.

Dani handed another blanket to Cole but he tossed it on the sofa. She looked up at him, her gaze filled with questions.

He telegraphed an I'll-tell-you-later look and went to the lamp. "We need to turn off the lights until I'm sure we're secure."

Dani didn't question him. He turned off the lamps, and she went for the wall switch.

He nodded at the bank of windows on the far side of the room. "Blinds next."

He grabbed the remote and set the blinds in motion on the floor-to-ceiling windows facing the ocean. The motor whirred, slowly bringing down the blinds but not before he caught sight of the two men trudging along the beach far too close to the house for comfort.

Cole glanced at Alyssa sitting wide-eyed on the couch, the blanket doing nothing to stop her shivering. He'd taken on the responsibility of protecting her, but was he up to the task if he couldn't put behind him the loss of his buddy in Iraq? A loss that was all Cole's fault.

Shake it off, he warned himself as he'd done

when he needed to finish out his last tour after Mac died.

"Take Alyssa to the hallway," he barked at his sister. "If we have a breach, take her out the garage door and evacuate."

Dani didn't hesitate but hurried to Alyssa and lifted her by the arm.

"What's happening?" Alyssa's voice rose in alarm.

"The men who were following you are heading toward the deck." Cole didn't have to say any more. The look on Alyssa's face said it all.

If he didn't somehow stop these men from getting inside and figuring out she was the one who overheard them, her life would be at stake—and his and Dani's, too.

TWO

Once in the long hallway, Alyssa shook off Dani's arm and peered around the corner. Framed in a shaft of light seeping through the small window from the outdoor security light, Cole stood at the ready. Alyssa could only gape at him.

He had a gun. A gun, for goodness' sakes! Apparently, he'd had it with him all this time. While he'd held her. While he'd carried her and she'd rested her head trustingly on his chest, he'd been armed like the men chasing her.

"Stay here." Dani shot across the room, surefooted even in the dim lighting, and joined her brother. She swooped down and pulled a weapon from an ankle holster, the grace and ease of the movement proving she'd done so many times before.

Seriously? Both of them had guns?

"Who are you people?" Alyssa asked, surprised at how shrill her voice sounded.

"All you need to know right now is that we're here to help you." Cole kept his intense focus on the window in the door.

Should she have blindly trusted a strange man on the beach? Had she traded one set of killers for another?

Neither of them looked like killers, and Cole had said he used to be a U.S. Marshal... but then Nolan was a cop and now she had reason to believe he'd murdered Todd.

Unbelievable!

How could she ever imagine when she'd set off tonight that the man who'd cared for them since Todd died was the one who'd ended Todd's life? Now she didn't know what or who to believe. Who to trust.

"Looks like they're moving down the beach," Cole said, grabbing Alyssa's attention. "Head upstairs, Dani, and keep an eye on them until they're out of sight."

Dani gave a clipped nod and Alyssa stepped back into the main room. Dani jogged to the open staircase on long legs that took her up the steps in a flash.

Cole lowered his gun, but kept it gripped between both of his hands and his focus on the door. Silhouetted by the outside light, his long-sleeved shirt clung to his body, molding to muscles she knew were rock hard from when he'd carried her to the house. He was tall—well over six feet she figured. She had to look up at him and she easily cleared five-eleven without shoes. Chestnut-colored hair covered his collar and had a slight wave as it started to dry.

"We're clear, Cole." Dani's voice came from upstairs, and Alyssa pulled her focus from him to watch Dani run down the stairs. "Go ahead and have a seat, Alyssa."

"Now would be a good time to tell me who you are and why you have guns." Alyssa directed her comment to Dani, who hadn't asked a single question of Cole. If Alyssa had a brother who brought home a soaked stray, she'd be peppering him with nonstop questions.

Dani just smiled, lighting up a beautiful face surrounded by natural blond waves. She clicked on a lamp, flooding the room with light. Alyssa blinked until her eyes adjusted; by that time Cole was joining her. His lips tipped in a warm smile. Instead of making Alyssa feel welcome the way Dani's had, it surprised her when her heart started beating a little bit faster.

She dropped onto the sofa and adjusted the blanket to hide her surprise.

"You okay?" He sat on the table facing her and set his weapon next to him.

"Yes." She looked into sharp blue eyes that missed nothing yet were kind. She felt a warm connection. Not an earth-shattering, startling sizzle—just a feeling that he was a good and honorable man.

"Alyssa," he said, breaking the spell and making her jump, "whatever's going on with you, we can help work through it. That's what we do and we'd gladly accept you as a client."

She watched him, searching for duplicitous motives. She found only kindness laced with something that resembled sorrow.

"A client?" she asked.

"Remember I told you I used to be a marshal?" Cole's gaze didn't waver. "Well, all of my brothers and sisters used to work in law enforcement, too. Now we operate a private investigations agency in Portland. We're a nonprofit agency that specializes in providing free services to people who are in need but can't afford quality investigators."

Private investigators? Maybe they could help her find out if Nolan killed Todd.

"Wait." Dani came forward and those questions that hadn't been asked earlier lingered on her face. "Alyssa's not a client?"

"Not yet," Cole said. "We just met on the beach, but it seems like she's a good candidate for our help."

"No wonder you were freaked out by our guns." Dani grabbed a laptop from the table and plopped onto the sofa. She typed for a few moments, then swiveled the screen toward Alyssa. "Here's our company Web site. This tells you a little about our family. Just so you know we're legit."

Thankful Dani seemed to be a mind reader, Alyssa focused on the About Us page on a professional Web site for The Justice Agency. The page contained no photos but held bios for each of them. Five siblings. Three men and two women. She scanned the page, aware that Dani and Cole were both watching her, but she wouldn't hurry and miss a single word. If she was going to consider letting them help her figure out if Nolan really had killed Todd, she had to be sure they were trustworthy.

She read the short family bio. Interesting. All of them were adopted, which explained how Dani could be blonde and fair-skinned next to Cole's swarthy complexion and darker hair. But they all did have law enforcement backgrounds, as Cole mentioned. Dani and Ethan Justice were experienced FBI agents. Kat and Derrick were former Portland police officers. And Cole was a former U.S. Marshal, like he'd said.

There were testimonials from clients gushing about the Justice family's ethics, compassion and top-notch abilities. All services were provided for free, assuming the client met their needs assessment.

Could her luck be changing? Had God heard her prayers and led her to a family who could help her?

"I'd really like to think you're good guys."

Alyssa tried to put strength she wasn't feeling into her tone.

"But something's stopping you," Cole added.

"It's just—" She paused to formulate her sentence so she didn't come off sounding ungrateful for their offer and didn't share too much about her situation until she was sure she could trust them. "The men chasing me are police officers, and unless I misunderstood what I overheard, they're drug dealers, too. So the fact that you once worked in law enforcement might be a big selling feature for potential clients, but not for me. Law enforcement backgrounds don't prove you're honest or trustworthy. Plus it can't be a good sign that all five of you left that line of work."

"We weren't kicked out, if that's what you're thinking." Cole chuckled, a cute dimple piercing his cheek.

Dani sat forward, her usual smile missing. "Our parents were murdered a few years ago and the police couldn't find the killer. We each took a leave of absence to find who was responsible. We discovered we liked working together, so we formed our agency."

"I'm so sorry about your parents," Alyssa said sincerely. She knew how hard it was to lose parents. Hers had died in a car wreck during her last year of college.

"Turning our focus on helping people in need has made the loss easier to handle." Dani closed her computer. "I don't know what's going on with you yet, Alyssa, but we'd be glad to help if we can." She squeezed Alyssa's hand.

After spending nine years married to a police officer and hanging around others in the profession, Alyssa had developed a discerning ability to weed out the fakes. At least she thought she had before Nolan revealed his secret tonight. Could she trust her instincts anymore?

Still, these people didn't appear to be fake. They seemed good, strong—amazing. Starting with Cole, who risked his life to bring her here, and extending to Dani, who let a stranger into the house without question. Tears threatened to flow as a result of their kindness, and she swallowed hard to hold them back.

She looked at Dani and kept her tone light.

"How can I turn down help from a woman who reacted so calmly when her brother dragged in a strange woman off the beach?" Alyssa forced out a chuckle to lighten the mood and glanced at Cole.

Abruptly he grinned, exposing that dimple in his left cheek again.

Oh, wow, she thought. *Wow.*

He was gorgeous. Absolutely gorgeous and would have women falling all over him. And that included her. The memory of being carried up the beach flashed into her mind. She'd felt safe and secure, like nothing could harm her. That was even more attractive than his smile.

How long had it been since she'd felt safe and cared for? Cherished? Had she ever truly felt that way with Todd? Not really. Not even before the night two years ago when in anger he'd hit her and she'd asked him to move out of the house, basically ending their marriage.

Dani cleared her throat, and the memory washed away like the mighty waves pounding the shore. The feeling of safety ebbed away with it.

This couple might want to help her, but she

still wasn't cared for. She'd known that since she and Todd split up, especially after he started hounding her at all hours of the day, wanting to get back together. She needed to keep remembering the way he'd failed her so this pair of amazing blue eyes still fastened to her didn't make her forget what she knew with a certainty.

Men couldn't be trusted.

No matter the first impression, no matter the connection, they all disappointed when it came to the important things of life. She just had to keep remembering Nolan's most recent betrayal, and she'd be able to avoid any man. Even this one who set her heart beating faster than it had in years.

Cole watched Alyssa. Something shifted in her eyes, making them dark and unreadable. It'd been a long time since he'd connected this strongly with a woman. Not since he'd received the Dear John letter in his first tour of duty two years ago. On his thirty-first birthday, no less. On that day he'd said goodbye to a potential wife and family. After the daily worry over his safety in Iraq, Laura said she couldn't handle having the same angst when he returned to his job as a U.S. Marshal, putting him in danger every day.

Now he was out of practice when it came to women. But not so out of practice that he didn't recognize interest when he saw it. Her eyes had heated up and flashed an awareness of him for a brief moment. Of that he was certain.

Now she just looked sad. Wounded. So wounded. And he wanted to help her. To find out what made her tick. To ask why she'd shut down so fast. But Dani was scrutinizing his every move the way a parent would watch a baby needing to be coddled. He didn't need more of that kind of scrutiny from his family. They'd had him under a microscope since he'd come home from Iraq. Maybe waiting for him to crack up and fall apart.

He would keep things professional and settle for finding out why Alyssa ended up on that rock with him in the middle of a winter storm. "If we're going to help you, we'll need to know what happened tonight."

"It's a long story," she answered vaguely.

Not unusual. Getting a client to share what

was frequently an emotional topic—or at the least very personal—was often the hardest part of helping them.

He sat back to give her more space and make her feel more comfortable. "We have time. Start at the beginning and be honest with us. No matter what the problem is, we won't judge you."

She looked warily at him and pulled the blanket tighter as if she felt a need to protect herself. He glanced at Dani. She'd already noticed Alyssa's uneasiness and had reached out to squeeze her hand.

"We've all made mistakes," Dani said. "Or have things in our lives we don't want to share with others. What you tell us stays with us and the rest of our family."

Alyssa squared her shoulders and that steely resolve he'd seen at the beach returned to her face. "I guess it started when my husband died."

A husband, huh? Unexpected.

No way Cole would've missed seeing a wedding ring, but he glanced at her hand to be sure. Just like he'd thought. Her finger was bare and didn't have a telltale circle from recent wear, meaning her loss happened a while ago.

"He was a police officer," Alyssa continued. "He was found murdered in his patrol car. A bullet to his chest and a stash of meth in his possession. The sheriff's department investigated and when his tox screen came back positive for meth, they dug deeper. They discovered he'd worked as part of a drug ring. His role was to tell the rest of the organization when a bust was coming so they escaped arrest." She ran a hand over her face.

"That must've been hard to find out." Dani patted Alyssa's knee.

"It was, but then tonight I overheard his former partner, Nolan Saunders, basically admit to killing Todd and framing him with the drugs." Her tone was cool again, like the freezing rain that had pelted them on the beach, and she calmly recited the events. As if his death was of no consequence to her. But he saw the tremble of her hands and the pain in her eyes that she was trying desperately to hide.

"His partner?" Dani asked, a compassionate look on his younger sister's face. "Had you suspected him before?"

Alyssa wearily shook her head. Dani squeezed Alyssa's hand again.

Cole was grateful Dani was here. She was such a comforter, always ready to help others, and she was making this easier on Alyssa while he had to ask the hard questions. "How long has it been since your husband was killed?"

"Two years." Alyssa clasped her trembling hands together. "That's when Nolan really got involved in our lives. He said he'd promised Todd he'd look after me and the kids."

"So you have children," Dani said.

Alyssa's smile softened, her expression melting with love. She wasn't at all the detached woman she'd tried so hard to portray tonight. "Twins. A boy and girl. They're seven. They're at home with my friend Paula." Alyssa shifted on the sofa. "I really should call her to tell her I'm running late."

Dani grabbed a notepad. "Give me her number, and I'll let her know you're with us so you can keep telling Cole about what happened."

Alyssa rattled off the number, and Dani stepped a few feet away to call.

"You were saying that Saunders helped you and the twins out," Cole said, hating the thought of a killer anywhere near this woman.

She nodded. "I only worked part time when Todd was alive. When he died, he left behind a mountain of debts, and after the investigation his death benefits were denied. We weren't left with much, but we had enough for me to renew my real-estate license." Her back went up again as if she needed to prove she could be strong. "We lived in one side of Nolan's duplex, and after Todd died Nolan let us stay there rent free. He also helps with the kids. He picks them up from school and watches them when I have to show properties outside school hours." She looked up and tears glistened in her eyes. "Now I don't know what I'll do."

Cole fisted his hands. He couldn't wait to investigate this Nolan guy and see that he paid for his crimes and for the way he'd hurt Alyssa. "So you believe Saunders is involved in the drug trade?"

"Yes. He was arguing with another officer,

Frank Gibson, who wanted out of their operation. Nolan said if Frank bailed on them, he'd end up a homicide statistic like Todd." She shivered under the blanket and tugged it tighter.

It wasn't hard to see how afraid Alyssa was of Saunders, but this statement by the officer wasn't proof that Saunders had killed her husband. Saunders could simply be using the homicide to build his street cred.

"But he didn't actually say he killed Todd," Cole clarified.

"No. It was implied. As much as I don't want to believe he killed Todd, I think he did. Plus Frank sounded upset. Like he was worried they'd kill him, too, if he tried to bail on them."

"So how did they end up chasing you?" Dani asked as she rejoined them.

Alyssa looked at Dani. "Is Paula okay with me being late?"

Dani nodded. "She'll stay as long as you need."

"So about the men, how'd you see them?" Cole asked, bringing them back.

"I'm a runner. I don't usually run in the

evenings, but I overslept this morning. I had a stressful day and I called Paula to watch the kids so I could run it off. I decided to take the scenic trail overlooking the beach to tire myself out before bed. That's when I heard them arguing on the path below me. After I heard what they'd said, I tried not to make any noise as I headed for my car. But I fell and that alerted them that I was there. When they came after me, I ran."

Cole thought about the men at the beach and their conversation. They never mentioned specifically looking for Alyssa. Not even looking for a woman. They'd just used the words "person" and "anyone." "And did they know it was you?"

"When Nolan told the other men to chase me, he said get *him,* so I don't think he knows it was me." She shivered. "Now I don't know what's going to happen to us. I mean, what do I do? I can't report what I heard to the police department. Nolan's father is the police chief. The whole department could be involved in this for all I know." Her teeth started chattering.

Police chief? Well, that raised the stakes

and made this even more complicated. Cole wanted to keep questioning her, but he had enough information to begin a preliminary investigation, and she should get home to her kids and out of her wet clothes.

"You don't need to do anything, Alyssa." Cole made eye contact with her, making sure she knew they were here for her. "We'll investigate both Todd's murder and Saunders's connection to any drug activities. As a bonus, we might even be able to clear Todd's name and get his death benefits reinstated."

"That would be great," she said.

"The best thing now is for one of us to take you home. You'll have to act like everything is normal and pretend nothing happened."

"I need to get my car first." Alyssa suddenly looked exhausted. "It's in a public lot downtown."

An alarm bell rang in Cole's head. "Any chance that could lead them to you?"

"I suppose it's possible, but if Nolan asks, I can always say I was meeting a client to show a house."

"Sounds like a good plan," Cole offered. "We'll get your car on the way to your house.

And on the drive we can talk about what to say in case Saunders asks any questions about tonight. Okay?"

Alyssa simply answered with a resigned nod.

"We can't have you going home looking like that and claiming you were showing houses." Dani stood and pulled Alyssa to her feet. "Let's get you into some dry clothes first." Dani gave Cole a pointed look and tugged on his shirt. "You might want to clean up, too."

As they left the room, he realized how cold he was. When he'd given his coat to Alyssa, the rain had soaked him through, yet he'd never really felt the chill. Not until now. Until she'd left the room, giving him time to think about what had occurred tonight.

If he hadn't been on the beach searching for the way out of his funk, these men might've found her. Or she could've died from exposure. Either way there was a potential killer out there who had law enforcement training and skills. Skills that could help him figure out he'd been tracking Alyssa tonight. And skills that would allow him to take her life just as he had her husband's.

THREE

Cole sat at the kitchen counter and waited for Alyssa and Dani to return. When he'd gone to his room to change, he'd heard the guest shower running. Likely at Dani's insistence. He smiled when he imagined his tenacious sister directing Alyssa to take a quick shower to warm up even though she wanted to get home.

He'd considered a short shower himself but decided against it and simply slipped into dry clothes as he was eager to take care of his first order of business. He needed to run a background check on Nolan, Todd and Alyssa. As a former police officer, his brother Derrick was the perfect person to do it.

He dug out his phone and dialed Dani's twin.

"So you *are* alive," Derrick answered, his tone filled with sarcasm.

Cole felt a moment of guilt. The family had decided he needed to take time off and work through the baggage he still carried from his two tours in Iraq. Miffed at their interference, he'd taken off to the beach and hadn't reported in for a few weeks. As the mediator of the family, Dani was dispatched here yesterday to make sure he was okay.

"I figured Dani would've called you all by now," Cole said.

"She did, but there's nothing like hearing your voice to prove you're still alive." This time Derrick's voice held brotherly concern instead of sarcasm.

Cole felt bad for making them worry. He just didn't know how to get a grip on the emotions he still battled. When the family had interfered, it had made him mad that he wasn't strong enough to shake it. In the end, he'd made things worse. "Look, man, I'm sorry. You know."

"I know," Derrick said. "So what's up?"

As Dani joined him in the kitchen, Cole told his brother about Alyssa's problem. "I need you to drop everything and do a background check on them. I'll text you with their info."

"Sorry, bro. I'd like to help, but Ethan's already got me on an assignment."

Cole sighed. As the oldest sibling, Ethan had taken charge of the agency and set their priorities. Normally, Cole didn't mind talking with Ethan, but he'd been all happy and gushy after getting married lately and that rubbed salt into Cole's wounds. A conversation with Ethan would only remind him of all he'd lost when Laura decided to bail on him right before their wedding.

Still, he wasn't going to give up on doing what was right for Alyssa just to avoid Ethan. "Is what you're working on a life-or-death matter?"

"No. It's a routine check for one of our business clients." To allow them to work most of their cases for free, they performed background checks for a long list of paying companies.

"Then I'll clear this with Ethan," Cole promised. "Any chance you can get started tonight?"

Derrick snorted. "You're pushing your luck here, bro."

"I know, but in a town this small one misstep could cost lives. We need to be prepared for anything."

"Who do you want me to start with?"

"Nolan Saunders."

"Fine. I'll call you as soon as I have anything to report." He disconnected and Cole stowed his phone in his pocket.

Dani finished pouring a cup of coffee and held up the pot. "You want a cup?"

He nodded.

She handed him the steaming mug. "I'll take care of getting Ethan on board."

No one ever volunteered to talk with Ethan about a change in agency priorities. Cole watched her carefully to see what she was up to.

She simply laughed. "What?"

"You're volunteering to talk to Ethan. What gives?"

"He's been more mellow since he got married. Plus I like Alyssa. Really like her, and for some reason I feel compelled to go the extra mile for her."

Me, too, Cole thought and instantly tamped it down. He'd known her for only a few hours, and he was acting like a schoolboy with a crush. Not only was it foolish behavior for a grown man, but it was foolish for him in particular when he hadn't worked out all his baggage from Iraq.

"Sounds like you think this case is going to be tricky." Dani slipped onto a stool next to him.

"We'll have to be careful." He set his mug on the counter and cupped his hands around it to warm them. "We're all used to working in a big city where anonymity is pretty much a given. Pacific Bay is a small town and gossip gets around."

"Then we'll need a cover story," Dani said.

"Alyssa mentioned showing houses tonight as an excuse for her car in the lot, so I can pose as one of her clients looking for rental property here. That'll give me a reason to ask questions without drawing attention. Plus I'll be able to meet with her on a regular basis and not raise Saunders's suspicion."

"You think he could have identified her tonight?"

"I don't know—maybe." He lifted his cup and took a long drink.

"You have great instincts, Cole. If you think it's possible, maybe it is."

"I keep thinking about the beach. It didn't take me long to recognize she was a woman by the way she carried herself. It wouldn't be farfetched to think the cops chasing her could've done the same thing."

"Maybe they didn't study her quite as carefully as you did." She ended with a wink.

He peered over his mug at her. "What's that supposed to mean?"

"I'm just saying something's going on with you that I haven't seen in a long time. I think, my dear brother, that you're interested in her."

He thought to deny it, but there was a good possibility that he was. Still, he didn't want to talk about it. "In case Saunders has identified her, we'll need to keep an eye on her until we're sure she's in the clear."

"Oh, yeah." She gave him a playful punch to the arm. "You'll keep an eye on her, all right. Both of them."

He rolled his eyes. "I'm serious, Dani."

"And that's why you've been exiled out

here. To get over this serious phase and let the Cole we all know and love come back."

"You'll have to get used to the new Cole. The old one is never coming back." He tweaked her nose. "I saw too much in Iraq for that to happen."

"That's a given, but the new Cole could still stand to laugh and smile a little more often."

He'd tried that. For two years. But it was hard to be lighthearted when his buddy was buried in the ground because of him.

From the corner of his eye, Cole saw Alyssa enter the room and he swiveled to face her.

"A smile like the cute one you have on your face right now," Dani whispered.

"Cute?" Cole groaned and watched Alyssa make her way across the open space. His assessment on the beach was right on target. She was gorgeous and regal-looking. Perfect posture. Slender, yet curvy in Dani's clothes. Her shoulder-length hair falling in soft waves framed her face.

"Wow. You clean up nice," Dani said to Alyssa while nudging Cole in the shoulder. He checked to see if his mouth was hanging open.

It wasn't, but he didn't know why not.

A man would need to be half-dead not to respond to this amazing-looking woman. And the way his heart was picking up speed proved he wasn't half-dead by any measure.

So what? He was just being a man. That's all there was to this. At least that's what he was telling himself. And would keep telling himself to get through this investigation without falling for her. No woman deserved to be saddled with his baggage. Especially not a woman who had her own share of problems.

But that didn't mean he'd leave her to fend for herself. He wouldn't let anyone get to her. Especially not the two-faced killer Nolan Saunders.

Alyssa shifted on the heated leather seat of Cole's SUV. She hugged the plastic bag holding her running gear in her arms and her car key snug in her palm. Cole and Dani had just walked her through the steps they'd take in their investigation, and she couldn't be more impressed with their skills.

Still, while they'd talked she'd kept her eyes on the road, watching for Nolan's police vehicle. She hoped he hadn't discovered her part in tonight's chase, but if he hadn't she couldn't help but believe it was only a matter of time before he did. He was a good investigator. The best, Todd had said many times. She felt her discovery was imminent.

"You're awfully quiet, Alyssa," Dani said from the backseat. "Do you have any questions about our plan?"

"Are you sure there's nothing I can do to help resolve this?" Alyssa swiveled toward Dani but met Cole's gaze as he sat behind the wheel.

He spent a long moment studying her before turning back to the road. "Just go about life as normal unless I tell you otherwise."

Normal, right! "I don't know if I can do this, Cole." She worked hard to keep her tone level even though she felt panic trying to elevate it. "I don't think I can even look at Nolan again, much less pretend he's the same man I once thought he was."

Dani leaned forward. "Is it likely you'll see him often in the next few days?"

Alyssa nodded. "We talk every day. In fact,

if my lights are on tonight, it wouldn't be unusual for him to stop in when he gets home."

"I doubt he'll be home soon," Dani said. "Since his mystery eavesdropper got away, he's likely meeting with his men to do damage control."

"I suppose," Alyssa replied, but she didn't take much comfort from Dani's statement. "But what about tomorrow? He's bound to want to talk me. Especially after his announcement last week."

"What announcement?" The intensity of Cole's gaze unsettled Alyssa even more.

"He hinted at us becoming more than friends and he's waiting for me to give him the green light on a relationship. Not that I ever intended to pursue anything with him, but I couldn't think of a good way to let him down."

"Hopefully his feelings for you won't complicate things," Cole said.

Hoping the same thing, Alyssa sighed and returned her focus to the window. The heavily forested roadside disappeared, signaling their arrival in the city limits.

Retail establishments lined both sides of the

highway. Once they turned off and headed into the downtown area the shops sat closer together and antique street lamps cut through the fog and spilled over the brick streets.

Cole slowed and tipped his head at a parking lot on the right. "Is this the lot?"

"Yes."

He pulled into the main downtown parking lot, still filled with employees and diners' cars. Even in the inclement winter months, the town's population swelled with tourists seeking off-season rates. Several couples hurried through the drizzle to their vehicles, but there was no sign of Nolan.

"Which car is yours?"

"The blue SUV. Third car from the building."

Cole pulled up behind her car and left his vehicle idling. Dani popped open her door and slid out. She was going to drive Cole's car while Cole rode with Alyssa, making sure she got home safely. She stood outside Alyssa's door, watchful and searching, her hand on the handle.

Alyssa looked at Cole, once again thankful for his expertise. "Are you sure you don't mind driving me home?"

"I don't mind in the least." He smiled, his dimple winking at her.

She could sit and stare at his smile all night. There was something special about how his face lit up, yet it seemed like he didn't share a smile with just anyone, making her feel special. How she could go from fearing Nolan in one second to melting at a smile the next was beyond her. She forced herself to look away and push open her door.

Alyssa started to slide out and Dani stepped into her path, keeping her in the car. "We'll wait for Cole to check out your car."

He searched every conceivable hiding space while walking around Alyssa's SUV. He held himself with a confidence she was beginning to realize was part of who this man was. He opened the driver's-side door and checked the interior. Then, still standing, he reached in, started the engine and stepped back. Odd.

"I've never seen anyone start a car like that," Alyssa commented more to herself than to Dani.

"It's a safer way to do it if someone has tampered with your vehicle."

Alyssa's gaze flew to Dani's. "Is that even possible? You said it was unlikely that Nolan knew it was me."

"It is unlikely but not impossible." Dani smiled, but her hand drifted to the weapon she had holstered on her belt, negating the smile. "Once you get to know Cole, you'll learn that he's thorough and doesn't take chances."

"So you think this is overkill?"

"*I* do, but then I never had to see what he's seen as a member of an elite squad during two tours of duty." Dani sighed and it carried the weight of the world.

Alyssa wanted to ask her about it, but Cole came over to them. He stopped in front of his sister but continued to scan the area. "We're good to go. You'll follow us?"

"Yes," Dani answered.

Surprised, Alyssa looked at Dani. "I thought you were going back home, but now that you mention it, Cole will need a ride from my place."

"It's not only that, but he also wants to make

sure you aren't tailed." Dani stepped behind the opened door.

Cole slipped his hand around Alyssa's elbow to help her down from the car. Though she didn't need his help, she didn't argue. He kept her close to his side and when they passed Dani, he shared a quick fist bump with her. They seemed so comfortable and in tune with one another.

Alyssa had always wanted a sibling to share this kind of camaraderie, but her parents didn't want a second child. She'd hoped for a large family with Todd—lots of noise, laughter and love shared between many children—but the dream of having more children died when Todd hit her.

It felt odd to settle in the passenger seat of her own car and even stranger when Cole climbed behind the wheel. She supposed he was used to adapting to an ever-changing environment in his job. She wished she could adjust so quickly, but her nerves were fried.

Too tired to give directions, she pressed Go Home on her GPS and the woman's voice spouted the first set of directions.

"You really shouldn't have your home address programmed in your GPS." Cole adjusted the mirrors. "If someone stole your car, they'd know where you live."

With Dani's heads-up about his thorough nature, she wasn't surprised at his comment. "I'll change it tomorrow."

He turned and gave Dani a thumbs-up. Alyssa heard Dani back the car out of their way.

Cole turned to the front, smiling at her. "You ready to go?"

She peered into his eyes. Blue. Like the ocean on a summer day. He seemed so self-assured, yet there was something lingering in the depths that belied the confidence. Nothing that made her doubt his abilities, but something she knew he was questioning, maybe searching for.

Their gazes met and held. His smile disappeared and his eyes turned dark and unreadable. He suddenly seemed too close for comfort and the car too small.

"I really should be getting home," she said and hated the way his expression became guarded, a feeling she knew all too well from her failed relationship with Todd. But that was a good thing, right? If he looked at her like this more often, reminding her to keep her distance, she wouldn't have to fight this crazy attraction.

He pulled out of the lot, and once on the road, she listened to the rhythmic *thump, thump* of the intermittent wipers, hoping the soothing sound would calm her nerves. The dashboard cast a red glow, and she could see Cole check the mirrors on a regular basis— maybe making sure Dani, and no one else, followed them. Neither of them spoke. The quiet, save the wipers and hissing sound of tires spinning over wet pavement, felt uncomfortable as could be expected between two strangers.

And they were strangers. They'd only met a few hours ago. But there was a connection between them, too. Even if she didn't like it, she couldn't deny it.

He followed the GPS instructions, making all the directed turns. They pulled onto her street, and she was thankful not to see Nolan's car in front of their nondescript box of a duplex. Each of them had a one-car garage, but Nolan had filled his with sporting equipment and had no room for his car so he parked on the street.

A single light brightened the front porch of her home. It was usually a beacon welcoming her home. But tonight the thick fog cloaked the shadows around the property, creating dark and murky places to hide.

"It would be best if we could park in the garage," Cole said, obviously on the same wavelength.

Thankfully, Paula's husband had dropped her off, so her car didn't block the driveway. Alyssa pressed the remote mounted on the visor. The garage door groaned and protested its age, then rumbled up. Cole expertly slid her large car into the tight space and turned off the motor.

Expecting Dani to join them, Alyssa glanced back, but Dani's car wasn't in the driveway or on the road. "Where's Dani?"

"We didn't want to risk Saunders seeing her if he was home. She'll be waiting for me a few blocks away."

"He isn't home. He parks on the street and his car isn't here." Just the thought of him nearby sent a shiver over her body. She couldn't imagine how she would've handled it if he had been here. She wrapped her arms around her waist.

"Hey." Cole laid a warm hand on her shoulder. "I won't let anything happen to you. In fact, I need to check your home to make sure everything's okay before leaving you alone."

Did he really think something had happened to Paula and the twins? Not likely. Nolan would never hurt the kids, would he? "If anything's wrong, Paula would call me."

He studied her for a moment, then drew in a deep breath. "There's something we need to get straight, Alyssa. If I'm to do my job and do it right, there will be things I have to do that aren't optional. This is one of them." His tone was sharp, his eyes dark. She suddenly felt sorry for Nolan if he ever crossed this man's path.

"And what am I supposed to tell Paula about you looking through my house?"

"Does she have any connection to the police force or Nolan?"

"Her husband's a police officer."

"Then for your own safety, we'll have to

use a cover story. Tell her I'm a client and you wanted me to see the layout of your place."

She didn't want to lie to Paula, but she'd do so for her children's safety. Without another word, she climbed out.

Cole went to the door leading into her house. As he pushed it open, he settled a hand on the weapon he'd holstered at his waist before leaving his rental house. Her concern rose not only for her own safety, but for her children, as well.

He seemed to shake it off, though, and held out his hand. Needing to check on her babies, she rushed inside without a backward glance to see if he followed. On the way to the stairs, she spotted Paula sound asleep on the sofa.

Breathing a sigh of relief for her friend's safety, Alyssa charged up the steps as sore muscles from her frantic escape from Nolan screamed at her to slow down. But nothing would stop her from making sure the twins were okay.

Cole caught up with her. "The point of me being here is to check things out before you run headfirst into danger."

"I just need to make sure the twins are fine."

His eyes softened a bit. "Which room is theirs?"

"Second door on the left," she answered. "Please be careful not to wake them."

"They won't even know I was here." He moved stealthily down the hallway, his footfalls silent and quick, almost as if he were one of the dark shadows outside. He slipped into the twins' room and she followed.

"Thank You, Father," she whispered at the sight of her babies safely in their twin beds.

Cole went straight to the window and closet, then knelt down to check under their beds. Alyssa was thankful she'd recently discovered Riley had been hiding kid's-meal boxes under his bed. Riley had wanted to use them as blocks to build a fort. Unfortunately, he hadn't removed all the food, and she'd found petrified French fries.

Cole came to his feet and paused between the twin beds to look down on Riley and Brianna. In the soft light coming from the hallway, Alyssa saw his face soften. He was such an enigma. Tough, strong, unyielding—and here he was smiling softly at her twins.

He suddenly shook off whatever he was feeling and turned. "Let me check the other rooms and then we can go back downstairs." He left the room as silently as he'd entered.

She went to Brianna's bed and tucked the blanket up to her chin. After running a hand over her soft curls, Alyssa kissed her daughter's forehead. She moved to Riley's bed and found his comforter decorated with colorful footballs dangling at the end. She tugged it up and pressed a kiss on his cheek. He stirred, then turned over and settled deep into the covers.

Thank You, Lord, for giving me these beautiful children, and keep us all safe through the night. Alyssa headed for the hall where she met Cole.

He held up a hand. "Wait here while I confirm the first floor is clear."

Knowing better than to try to argue, she sat down on the top step to wait. He returned in a few moments and motioned for her to join him. When she reached the first floor, she found him at the front door.

"Everything's secure," he whispered, likely to keep from waking Paula, and pulled open the door.

"So will I see you tomorrow?" she asked, suddenly feeling very alone.

"It'd be a good idea to get together for a status update. Where do you usually meet clients?"

"At my office or a coffee shop."

"If we meet for coffee you won't have to explain who I am to your coworkers."

"Good thinking." She gave him the location of the place she usually frequented. "Ten would be a typical time I'd meet a client."

"Then ten o'clock it is." He looked at her for a few moments, seeming to memorize everything about her. She figured with his skills he'd already done so, but this look was softer, as if he didn't want to leave her alone.

Touched by his kindness, she smiled her thanks. He pulled back, as if she'd branded him.

"If you need anything tonight," he stepped onto the porch, "I'll be standing watch outside."

She'd thought he'd drop her off and go

home. "I can't let you stay outside all night. Not in this weather."

"Trust me. I've had to stand duty in much worse."

She didn't want to impose on him any more tonight, but the iron resolve on his face said it was useless to argue, so she stood in the doorway until he disappeared into the foggy night.

As she reached for the door, she spotted Nolan's car turning onto her street. She quickly closed the door and locked it. She rushed through the room, turning out lights. Hopefully she'd snapped them off before Nolan discovered she was awake and stopped by to question her about the night.

FOUR

Cole stood behind a tree in the green space across from Alyssa's duplex. Cold, driving rain saturated his jacket, chilling him to the core, but he wouldn't leave Alyssa. Especially not with Saunders arriving home. Every muscle in Cole's body tensed as he watched Saunders roll down the driveway in his SUV with Pacific Bay Police emblazoned on the side. He parked in front of the shared duplex and turned off his engine.

Hand on his weapon, Cole scoped out the fastest path to Alyssa's home should Saunders knock on her door. Or worse, break through the door.

Dressed in jeans and a black jacket, Saunders climbed out of his vehicle. He headed up the walkway, the fog melding with his body and making him look far more dangerous than the picture Derrick had texted a moment ago.

Ready to intercept Saunders if he even hinted at going for Alyssa's home, Cole took a step, but an irritating rap song blared from Saunders's cell phone and he stopped to answer. With quiet once again restored in the neighborhood, Cole heard soft footfalls coming from behind. *Dani.* He slipped deeper into the shadows until he could be certain it was her.

She approached wearing a camouflage slicker, hood up, and Cole turned his focus back to Saunders.

"This better be important," Saunders said into his phone.

Dani silently took the spot next to Cole and handed him a slicker. Cole shrugged into the slippery vinyl, lifting the hood against the chilly rain.

"I pay you to work out these distribution problems," Saunders said, clearly irritated. "If you don't get the product distributed tonight, you'll be in a world of hurt."

Saunders suddenly spun toward his car. "Fine. I'm on my way, but if this happens again, you're history. You got that?" He clapped his phone closed and shoved it in his pocket. After a long look at the duplex, he shook his head and climbed into his cruiser.

"Tail him," Cole whispered without taking his focus off Saunders. "Don't let him out of your sight."

Dani slipped into the darkness like the hazy mist joining with the trees.

Cole stood at attention until Saunders's cruiser rolled past, then he settled back against the tree for a long night. His mind instantly went to Alyssa, her face, the terror in her eyes at the beach, the startling beauty when she'd cleaned up. She piqued his interest in a way no other woman had in years, but thinking about her in any way other than how to protect her was *not* where his mind needed to be when standing duty.

He fisted his hands and redirected his thoughts the way his military training had taught. Keep focused on the mission. Protect your team. See the desired outcome and block out everything else.

It had been quiet for hours when Cole heard a car slow on the road and turn onto the driveway. He moved deeper into the trees. An SUV with the same Pacific Bay Police logo slipped past. He couldn't get a good look at the driver, but it was likely Saunders returning home. The driver swung the car into a parking space, and Cole silently moved through the trees for a better look.

Saunders climbed out, carefully scrutinizing his surroundings before opening the back door of his vehicle. He bent inside and came out holding a small gym bag. Not likely workout clothes. Probably cash, drugs or weapons. Saunders moved toward his front door, his steps sure and certain yet hurried. The behavior of someone who feared discovery. Not that he had any clue Cole was out here, but engaging in illegal activities would keep Saunders on edge.

Cole watched until he saw the upstairs light on Saunders's side of the duplex turn on then off. A short hoot rang out, sounding so much like an owl only he would know Dani was the source of the sound. He went to meet her, and together they moved deeper into the heavily treed green space to talk.

"What happened?" he asked.

"Saunders met with another man." She lifted the front of her slicker and turned on a digital camera. She held her slicker out to keep the camera's light from shining through the darkness. "This is the guy. Wish I could've gotten a better picture, but I couldn't risk being seen so I had to shoot from a distance."

Cole bent down to look at the screen. "It's not your best work, but it might be clear enough for Alyssa to identify him. Send the picture to my phone, and I'll show it to her tomorrow."

Dani clicked the camera off. "I'll also send it to Jennie to clean up the focus. If we're lucky we'll get a match using facial recognition software." Ethan's wife, Jennie, was a professional photographer. She'd be the best-qualified person to work on the photo. Assuming Ethan let her get involved in a case.

"That would be great. If we know the kind of thugs Saunders is working with, we can create a better plan to protect Alyssa."

"I also grabbed a cigarette butt this guy tossed. I'll send it to Portland for DNA processing tomorrow."

"Hopefully he has a profile in the system." Cole didn't have to tell Dani that finding a match was a long shot. With DNA processing being so costly, criminal profiles weren't completed as frequently as law enforcement would like.

Dani took a step closer. "I've been thinking we should see if the DEA has an active investigation on Saunders."

"I thought about that, too."

"But?" She raised a brow.

"Even if they're investigating him, they may be going after someone higher up the food chain. In that case, they'd warn us off and that wouldn't help Alyssa at all."

"What if I could assure you that I'd be able to influence their investigation for our good?"

"And what gives you that assurance?"

Her lips tipped in a sly smile. "Let's just say I still have a DEA contact who owes me."

"And you're certain he'll play ball?"

She shrugged. "Certain? No. But I'm confident we'd at least be kept in the loop."

He peered at the dark windows on Saunders's side of the duplex. "We don't even know if Saunders ID'd Alyssa tonight. We're giving her 24/7 protection and she's safe for now. So let's see what the light of day brings and decide then."

"Sounds like a plan." Dani stretched her arms up high and rolled her head. "You want me to take the night shift?"

Nagging unease over failing to protect someone under his charge gnawed at his brain. He didn't want to leave Alyssa's protection up to anyone else. But if he didn't get some sleep tonight, he wouldn't be on top of his game tomorrow. With Saunders in bed for the night, he'd pose more of a threat tomorrow.

"It's all yours," Cole said. "I'm meeting Alyssa at ten. I'll take over her detail then. I shouldn't need you again until the evening so you'll be free to catch some sleep."

She took a step toward the house then turned back. "Other than getting that picture of Saunders from Derrick, did you hear anything from him on the background checks?"

"No, but with a mug like Derrick's I figured he needed his beauty sleep."

"Hey." She socked Cole's arm. "If you're

saying the man who looks like me is ugly, then you're saying I'm ugly, too."

Cole smiled and, even with the danger surrounding them, he couldn't believe how much lighter he felt inside than before coming to Pacific Bay. Like some of the pain from the past few years had lifted a bit. Maybe his siblings had been right. Maybe he'd needed this solitary time at the beach.

Maybe...but he wouldn't get his hopes up yet. Tomorrow was another day, and if his time in Iraq taught him anything, it was that life could explode in a matter of minutes and never be the same again.

Cole squinted at his phone in the morning sun and pressed redial for Alyssa. The call connected and went straight to voice mail as it had the last three times. Cole slammed a fist on the wheel and glanced at the clock. 10:05. He was already five minutes late for their meeting.

Five minutes. No big deal, right? Wrong. People could die in less than five minutes. People who were his responsibility. People he cared about.

"C'mon, move," he said to the traffic.

His phone rang and he punched talk without looking at the caller. "Alyssa?"

"Sorry, it's Dani."

"What's happening?" he asked with trepidation because Dani was still on Alyssa's protection detail.

"I have eyes on Alyssa. We're in the coffee shop parking lot. She was walking to the shop and Saunders rolled up."

Worry knotted Cole's stomach. "And?"

"And they're talking," Dani responded calmly. "You want me to intercede?"

A picture of Saunders grilling Alyssa about last night, grabbing her arm and dragging her off to kill her flashed into Cole's mind. He sucked in a breath to clear his thinking. "You have a read on their body language?"

"They're tense but not combative."

"Let them talk then, but move in if anything changes."

"You getting here soon?"

He looked at the unmoving vehicles. "Once I clear this intersection, I can take a side road and be there in five minutes."

As he disconnected, his heart flooded with

the horrible ache that had plagued him since he was in Iraq and hadn't gotten to Mac in time. He couldn't let anything happen to Alyssa on his watch. He had to act now. He cranked the steering wheel hard. His SUV jerked up and over the curb, grabbing the pavement on the other side and barreling down the alternate route to the shop.

He saw Alyssa standing with Saunders near the coffee shop. Dressed in his uniform, he had his hand clamped around her elbow, his posture rigid. The kind of stance assumed by an officer with an unruly suspect.

Jerking his car into the lot, Cole searched for Dani. She was well hidden, and it took a trained eye to find her. She stood at the ready if she needed to move and Cole knew she'd be on Saunders in a flash if he threatened Alyssa.

Even then, Cole didn't relax. Alyssa was his responsibility. His alone. He zipped into the nearest parking space and jumped from his car.

He caught Saunders's raised voice from a few establishments away. "So you're not avoiding me then?"

Alyssa sighed. "Why would I avoid you?"

"Because of what we discussed the other night."

Cole guessed he meant wanting to be more than friends with Alyssa, but Cole certainly wasn't going to ask the guy to clarify his comment.

"Alyssa," he said loudly as he approached. "Sorry I'm late."

She spun, her eyes going to his and filling with relief. "Oh, Cole, good. I was wondering if I'd gotten the time wrong for our meeting."

"I was held up by an accident blocking the road." He turned to Saunders, who let his hand fall from Alyssa's arm. "But then as a local cop you probably know all about it."

Saunders appraised him. "And you are?"

"Sorry." Alyssa shifted a folder and tablet computer she had clutched to her chest. "Cole is a new client." She looked up at Cole. "Cole, this is Nolan Saunders."

Proper manners dictated Cole stretch his hand out, but he couldn't shake hands with this man so he stood silently while Saunders continued to scrutinize him. "You're not from around here."

"Do I have tourist stamped all over me?" Cole kept his tone light to counteract the tension.

"Not hardly." Saunders's eyes narrowed in suspicion. "I make it a point to get to know all of our residents, and I haven't seen you around before."

"I'm looking for rental property."

"Oh, one of those." Disdain colored his tone, and Cole almost expected him to snarl.

Alyssa stepped closer to Cole. "If you'll excuse us, Nolan, we really need to get started if we're going to make our appointments."

Cole didn't wait for Saunders to bid them goodbye but backed away and pulled open the coffee shop door. Alyssa hurried past Cole, who stood his ground until she'd moved safely inside the shop.

Saunders fisted his hands and his focus never left Alyssa. His expression was wary, but when his eyes lifted to lock on Cole there was something more lurking in the depths. Ownership. Saunders was staking his claim to Alyssa and warning Cole off.

Cole returned the stare for a moment, making sure Saunders knew Cole was in control, then followed Alyssa into the shop. He slipped ahead of her to check out the room for potential threats. He could feel Saunders's gaze burning into his back and he forced himself to relax while looking for a table.

The small shop decorated with a nautical theme held six tables, and only one was vacant. Fortunately, it was secluded by the back door. He could talk to Alyssa without other patrons eavesdropping. He went straight to the table for two and pulled out a chair facing the wall so Alyssa didn't have to look at Saunders.

"I'll grab something to drink." Cole smiled, hoping to eliminate her unease. "What would you like?"

She didn't return his smile but sat woodenly, hugging her folder and computer. "Just coffee. Black, please."

On the way to the counter, he checked out Saunders in his peripheral vision. Cole was probably being overly cautious by not looking at the man directly, but police officers were suspicious of everything and everyone. Cole didn't want to give Saunders a reason to continue to watch them or, worse, do something impulsive. To be even more cautious, Cole wouldn't dismiss Dani from the parking lot until he was sure Saunders had departed.

Cole placed their order. As he waited for the barista to prepare it, he glanced at Alyssa. She was wearing a professional navy blue pantsuit with a crisp white blouse that brought out the deep brown of her eyes, making them large and luminous. She'd set her computer and folder on the table and clutched her hands in her lap.

"Your drinks," the barista said.

Cole grabbed the paper cups and took them to the table. "You look worried. Did Saunders say something?"

"No. Not really. But our conversation was tense." She removed the lid from her cup. "I couldn't tell if he'd figured out it was me last night, and that made it hard to look him in the eye. I think he suspects something."

"Explains why he's still watching us," Cole said. "It would help throw him off if you relaxed and acted like I'm a real client."

She nodded, but her back remained rigid. Cole needed to distract her. He tipped his head at her folder. "If you brought property listings we can pretend to take a look at them."

She pulled out a few flyers. She set them in front of him with trembling hands—he hoped Saunders didn't notice.

"Before we get started," she said, smoothing out a paper. "There's something important I need to tell you."

"Hold that thought until Saunders leaves."

Frustration flashed on her face so he quickly moved on by tapping the top paper. "This house looks amazing."

She ran a finger over the picture of a home with soaring windows overlooking the beach and her posture relaxed a bit. "This is my favorite property in the Pacific Bay area."

"Tell me about it." He smiled encouragingly and picked up his coffee.

"It has everything you could want. An open concept, modern kitchen that's to die for, lots of light, stunning views." She paused and smiled at him, the love for her job shining on her face.

"You really like being a Realtor, don't you?" he asked, hoping to keep her talking.

"I love helping people find a house that will

become their family home." Her eyes took on a faraway look. "I've always dreamed of what it would be like to own my own place. To make it warm and comfortable for my family." Her smile faltered. "At least I used to feel that way until Todd—" She cut herself off abruptly.

"And now?"

She lifted a shoulder in a shrug. "On my income, owning a house in this area is just a dream." She sounded so matter-of-fact about her limitations. So resolved. Yet not downtrodden by her circumstances.

Cole wished he could make her dream come true. Something he hadn't wanted to do for anyone in a very long time. When his dreams had died, he could no longer believe in other people's dreams, either.

"What about you?" she asked, warming to the subject. "Have you ever owned property?"

He shook his head. "I've never been in a position to settle down."

"Well let's pretend you want to settle down now and buy a house here. Would it be like the one you're renting?"

Would it? The main living area was warm and inviting. A place where a family could gather and spend time together. Or he could observe storms rolling onto the beach through the solid wall of windows facing the ocean. Windows that had put Alyssa at risk last night. People should never be at risk. At least not on his watch. "I like it okay, I guess."

"You guess, but what?"

"The windows would make the house hard to defend," he answered and noticed Saunders departing.

Alyssa suddenly sat back looking like he'd slapped her. "I should've known."

What had he said to make her change so quickly? "Known?"

"That you'd think about safety first." She looked away. "I mean, it's obvious from the chair you chose to sit in and the way you've been watching every little movement around us that you think like a cop."

Most civilians weren't that observant, but she'd pegged him. One hundred percent pegged him, and she hardly knew anything about him.

Alyssa laughed, but it didn't sound amused.

"Don't look so surprised. I was married to a cop, remember. I know all you law enforcement types like to sit facing the door and continually assess your surroundings. Never relaxing, even at home."

She'd lived the life many police officers' wives couldn't handle. A life his ex-fiancée, Laura, had refused to try. "Sounds like being married to a cop was hard for you."

She took a long sip of her coffee, as if needing time before answering. "It wasn't all bad. In fact, it was pretty good until the last couple of years. But right after his seventh anniversary on the job, Todd changed and things... well, things got tough."

Unfortunately, Cole had seen police officers lose their belief in their ability to make a difference on the job and start hating their work. That did not make for a good home life.

Cole opened his mouth to probe a little deeper, but Alyssa snapped the folder closed and the vulnerability in her eyes disappeared with it.

"So enough about me." She forced a laugh. "Is Nolan still watching?"

She'd completely shut down. Her refusal to

share hurt, surprising Cole. In less than a day, she'd somehow gotten through the wall he'd erected to keep people at bay and he sincerely wanted to get to know her. Problems and all. But her reluctance was probably a good thing. He didn't need to get involved with a woman who'd already experienced life married to a man with a dangerous job. She'd clearly hated that life and if Cole ever did consider a relationship with a woman, she'd need to accept his chosen career.

"Saunders is gone," he said and tried to ignore the return of her worried expression.

"Good. Then I can finally tell you that I lost my phone last night when I was running from Nolan. We need to find it before he does and figures out I was the one who overheard them."

Cole sat forward. "Are you sure you had it with you?"

"Positive. I never go running without my phone. When I went to get it out of my jacket this morning, it wasn't there. I called my number and it went straight to voice mail. I'm guessing the battery died."

"Which means if it has GPS, we won't be able to track it."

"Right. I even checked the emergency app I installed that will find a lost phone. Nothing." She shivered again.

"Maybe the rain damaged the phone."

"Even if it did, Nolan could still take out the SIM card and put it in another phone."

"SIM card," he said as he searched his limited knowledge of technology for a reason why the card was important. "That's the little card the phone company puts in the phone, right?"

"Right. It holds your personal details, like your name, phone number, et cetera. If Nolan put it in another cell, it would display my information."

This was not good news. Not good at all. Saunders was sure to have men processing the area hoping to find a lead that would give him the identity of the person who'd overheard them last night.

"Dani's a computer whiz. She might know of another way to locate your phone." He dug out his cell and dialed, then turned on his speaker so Alyssa could join in the conversation.

"Please tell me you're calling to say I can finally go get some sleep," Dani answered, sounding exhausted. "I'm getting too old to stay up all night."

"You're on speaker, Dani. Alyssa can hear you." Cole could almost see Dani blushing with embarrassment over a comment she'd never make in front of a client.

But he was more concerned by the guilty look stealing over Alyssa's face. "I'm so sorry, Dani. It's my fault you were up all night."

"No need to apologize," Dani replied. "So what's up, big brother?"

"We have a quick question for you." He lowered his voice and explained Alyssa's phone dilemma. "Is there any way to track the phone if the battery's dead?"

"No, sorry."

"Really, there's nothing you can do?" Cole asked.

"Only if someone finds the phone and charges the battery. In that case if the right app is installed, an email would be sent to notify us of the phone's GPS coordinates." Dani paused to draw in a breath. "Do you know the name of the app you installed, Alyssa?"

Alyssa rattled off the name.

"Good choice," Dani said. "That's the one I've installed on all the Justice Agency phones. It will definitely notify you if the phone is charged and turned on."

"It's just a matter of time before we know where the phone is," Cole said.

Alyssa's gaze shot to his. "How can you be so sure?"

"If Saunders finds it, he'll be sure to charge it to see who it belongs to."

Alyssa shivered and panic filled those amazing chocolate-brown eyes.

"Right, so Alyssa," Dani added, "if you want to email me the login information for your phone and the app, I'll be happy to check it out and monitor the phone."

"I can't keep you from your sleep."

"Hey." Cole peered at Alyssa. "This is why we're here. Besides, Dani lives for technology issues."

"He's right," Dani added. "I'm a total geek and proud of it."

"Okay, if you're sure."

"I'm sure."

"I have my computer here and can send you an email right now." Alyssa picked up her tablet and woke it up.

Dani rattled off her email address.

Cole waited until Alyssa had entered Dani's contact information, then he turned back to his phone. "Do you mind hanging around until I get Alyssa safely in the car and out of the lot?"

"No problem," she answered cheerfully, but he heard her stifle a yawn.

"Okay, Dani," Alyssa said. "The email is on its way."

"I'll set it up so the second someone powers up your phone, I'll get an alert."

"Thanks, sis." Cole hung up and caught Alyssa's concerned expression. "Is there something else?"

"I was thinking. Maybe we should try to look for my phone."

Cole shook his head. "Not a good idea. First of all, you can't be certain exactly where you lost the phone—finding it would be tough, even if we could be sure it's still there. And second, Saunders will have his men processing that area looking for any leads to your identity. We'd raise his suspicions if we showed up."

"How can you be so sure he'll do that?"

"Because that's what anyone in law enforcement would do."

"We have to do something. Nolan said he tried calling me last night and kept asking why I didn't answer. I told him my phone was dead. If we can't find it, at the very least I need to get a new one before he calls again."

Cole couldn't agree more. Since Saunders was already suspicious, he would call. Soon. It looked like the phone store was the next item on their agenda, and one they needed to take care of fast.

FIVE

Alyssa followed Cole to the coffee shop door. She forced a smile to her face and greeted her fellow residents with curiosity burning on their faces. Pacific Bay was a small town in the off-season and residents noticed things they were often too busy to see in peak tourist season.

"Stay here." Cole stepped onto the sidewalk.

Alyssa waited inside but not patiently. She wanted to get to the phone store before Nolan called again. The last thing she needed was for him to have another reason to seek her out. She'd told Cole she'd been uneasy in her conversation with Nolan, but the truth was, she'd barely kept it together and she was certain Nolan was suspicious.

Cole motioned for her to join him. "It's clear."

She felt the other patrons' eyes on them just as she'd felt Nolan watching her, so she hurried out the door and headed in the direction of her car. The sooner she was out of the public eye and they got on the road, the better.

"This way." Cole caught her arm and reversed her direction.

Feeling his hand clamping on her arm sent visions flashing into her mind of the night Todd hit her. He'd grabbed her in the same way, then lifted his other hand and slapped her. The memory real, vivid, and simmering just below the surface, she jerked her arm free. Her breath came in short pulses as she stared up at Cole and found him looking down on her, his face alive with questions.

"My car is the other way." He took a step closer to her, but she moved back.

"I'll drive."

"Not a good idea," he responded, but let his hand drop.

"You said we needed to make our cover story look legit. When I show houses, either I drive my clients or they follow me.

If Nolan finds out I've deviated, he'll know something's wrong."

"You never let clients drive?"

"Not usually."

"But you *have* let a client drive?"

"Once when I had car trouble."

"And did Saunders know about that?"

She nodded. "He arranged to have my car towed and repaired."

"Then you're about to have car trouble." He scanned the area again. "No more arguments. My car's right over there." He put his hand on her back and gently pressed her forward.

She didn't want to comply, but people were openly staring now and failing to follow his directive would only draw more attention. She allowed him to guide her to his SUV.

As he clicked his remote for the locks, she looked up at him, conveying her displeasure. "I'd like to talk about this, Cole."

"Let's get out of the open, and I'll explain. If you don't like my explanation, I'll reconsider letting you drive." At least he was open for discussion—something Todd never entertained when he was in one of his moods.

She climbed in. "You don't really think I'm in danger out here in broad daylight, do you?"

He slammed the door without answering, but she caught the worry in his expression before he hurried around the SUV. Maybe he believed Nolan had learned she'd overheard him last night.

Cole slipped in, put the key in the ignition and fired up his SUV, the large engine roaring from his aggressive foot on the gas pedal. Something had him spooked, and her anxiety mounted.

If he had any information about her situation, she needed to know. "Even if Nolan has figured out it was me last night, he's not foolish enough to try to hurt me in broad daylight in the middle of a busy shopping center." She met Cole's gaze directly. "And I'm pretty sure you know that. So why the big push to get me off the sidewalk? Unless, of course, you know something you're not telling me."

"I'm not withholding anything."

"I can't stand being lied to, Cole," she said, putting every ounce of feeling over Nolan's recent betrayal in her words. "If you're not going to be up front with me, then I'll have to find someone else to help me out of this mess."

"I'm not sure why you think I've lied to you, but I haven't and I wouldn't." His eyes flashed with hurt. "Ever."

"Then why this crazy reaction to walking to the car?"

He took a breath and held it then slowly eased it out.

A flicker of apprehension coursed through her. "What aren't you telling me?"

"Nothing. At least nothing to do with you. I… It's just…bad things can happen. Even when it doesn't seem possible. I'm responsible for your safety, and I can't let my guard down. Not for a second." She could feel his unspoken pain radiating across the cab.

"You're speaking from experience, aren't you?"

He nodded, but the movement of his head was so slight that if she hadn't been studying him intently, she wouldn't have seen it. Someone he cared about had been hurt, and he blamed himself. He didn't want the same thing to happen again so he'd overreacted.

Her anger melted away, but she still needed

an explanation for why she couldn't drive her own car. "I still don't get why I couldn't drive. We wasted time out there arguing when I would've gotten out of the open even faster if we'd gone straight to my car."

"From what you've said, it looks like Saunders is suspicious of you. That means he's made plans to track you. He knows your car and can have his fellow officers keep an eye out for you. But he doesn't know my vehicle—nor do they—so we won't be followed." He met her gaze again. "If I'm to keep you safe, we have to think like Saunders and remember he's not the man you once thought he was."

She didn't need any reminders of Nolan's betrayal. Her neighbor. Her friend. The man who'd held her children. Loved them, or seemed to, and watched over them, all the while knowing he'd killed their father. The thought of him holding Brianna and Riley sent a shudder down her back.

"Alyssa," Cole said, pulling her back. "Are we good to go?"

She nodded and looked out the passenger window, taking comfort in the familiarity of the shopping center, giving her hope that she would return to a normal life once this was over.

"Then a quick call to Dani and we're out of here," Cole said.

She heard him moving, digging out his phone and settling it in the dashboard holder, but she didn't want to look at him and reopen their discussion. Feeling lost and confused, she closed her eyes.

Father, please help me make sense of what's happening. I know You're here with me. Watching over me. Help me let go of my worry. To stop focusing on these problems that I know You will solve and to put my focus solely on You.

"Hey, sis," Cole said, bringing Alyssa's prayer to a close. "Alyssa needs to have a flat tire. Can you take care of it before you head home?"

Alyssa spun to look at him. He'd said she needed to have car trouble, but she never thought he'd actually make it happen.

Dani and Cole talked through the details of damaging her tire to make it look like Alyssa had picked something up on the road. Their back-and-forth discussion seemed as normal for them as if he'd called and asked her to stop at the store for a gallon of milk, not to slash a tire.

"Once you're done with that, get some sleep and I'll talk to you later." Cole pressed a finger on his phone, then pointed out the window. "There's Dani. Your tire will be flat in a few minutes."

Alyssa shook her head. "If you hadn't told me she was in the lot, I wouldn't even know she was here."

"If we do our job right, no one sees us." His expression suddenly turned serious. "Just remember—if we can tail you undetected, so can Saunders."

Not knowing how to respond, she stared ahead and waited for Cole to back out of the lot.

But he turned to her instead. "So the phone store. Care to give me directions?"

The space thick with tension, she searched for something lighthearted to ease the stress. "You're sure you want directions?"

"Yeah, why?"

"Well, you are a man, after all." She smiled at him.

He rolled his eyes then grinned. "Trust me. I'm secure enough to let a woman give me directions."

He really was secure. At least enough to make fun of himself. He'd just moved up a notch on her good-guy list.

"The only phone store in the area is at the downtown shopping center."

"Where you parked last night?"

She nodded and he maneuvered the truck out of the lot. She noticed him frequently checking the mirrors and glancing around, obviously looking for Nolan or one of his men.

Once on the main road, he seemed to relax a notch and pointed at his phone. "After Saunders came home last night he went out again and Dani followed him. He met with a man we think is involved in the meth distribution. Dani was able to snap his picture. It's not real clear, but if you grab my phone you can take a look at it to see if you know him."

Not really wanting to see this picture, she reached for the phone anyway and thumbed through the menus until she located his image folder. She opened the photo. Cole was right. The picture was dark and grainy, but she could still see the man had a thick head of dark hair, a wide jaw and mean-looking eyes.

"I don't know him, and I'm glad I don't." She shuddered.

"Dani also picked up a cigarette butt he dropped. We'll get it processed for DNA."

She settled the phone back in the holder. "That's good news then, isn't it?"

"Could be. But in order for the lead to pan out, the guy would've had to have been arrested and his DNA collected so it's a long shot."

Long shot or not, it was a lead and she would cling to the hope that it was a good one. "I'll pray that it works out."

He glanced at her. "So you're a woman of faith then?"

She nodded. "What about you?"

He shrugged. "God and I have been on a break for a while."

She understood that sentiment. She'd given up on God after Todd died until she figured out He was her key to moving forward.

Maybe Cole had walked away after losing the person he'd alluded to earlier.

Perhaps she could repay him for being here for her by helping him work through his loss. "If you ever want to talk about it, let me know."

Their eyes met for the briefest of moments. She caught another glimpse of his pain before he masked it. "We're here."

Ah, yes, he was avoiding the subject. That was his right. He swung his large vehicle into the lot, and parked in front of the phone store.

"Stay here while I check things out." He reached for the door handle then made his way around the front of the car.

The sun darted out from behind clouds and heavy shadows cast from brightly colored awnings clung to the buildings. Cole's focus was as sharp as a razor, searching every nook and cranny of the shopping center.

Seeming satisfied with what he'd seen, he opened her door. "We weren't tailed, but if Saunders has your phone, it wouldn't be a stretch for him to figure out you'd need a new one. Since this is the only store in the area, he could be concealed nearby. Stay close to me until I give the all-clear."

And just like that, the fear from last night returned with a force that threatened to swamp her. Looking around, searching the shadows, it took everything she had to climb out of the car and potentially reveal herself to a killer.

Cole peered out the phone store window, inspecting each vehicle turning into the parking lot. Alyssa had requested the same phone model as her current one and the sales rep was inputting her information into the computer.

"This'll take a few minutes if you want to look around at our accessories," the salesman said, and Cole heard the hope of add-on sales in his tone.

"Thanks," Alyssa replied and then joined Cole, a look of utter consternation clouding her beautiful face.

"Everything okay?" he asked.

"Buying a new phone isn't in the budget right now, that's all. No biggie." She smiled up at him.

He had to admire her attitude. She'd been thrown some curveballs in life, yet he could tell she tried to look on the bright side of things. That was not the way he'd been thinking about life at all since coming back from Iraq.

"I wouldn't need this new one if I could come up with when I lost it." She stared out the window, deep in thought. He stood silently by her side, listening to the computer keyboard click behind them.

"That's it." She glanced up at him. "I fell last night on the main jogging trail. I'm guessing my phone dropped out then."

"Then I need to get Dani out there in case Saunders hasn't come up with it."

"But you said Nolan would already be doing that and we couldn't go there."

Cole dug his phone from his pocket. "*We* can't because Saunders and his men know you. But since the odds are good that the phone is there, we need to take the risk of sending Dani to look for it. She'll come up with a cover story for being in the area, and she'll be discreet."

Alyssa shook her head. "I don't get how

you can be so calm. If I had the task you're giving Dani, I'd be so nervous I'd give myself away."

"It's simple really. We're trained to do it."

"Training aside, you need a certain personality to do what you do." Her wary tone showed her aversion to such a personality type and Cole knew without a doubt Todd had caused her to shy away from men in law enforcement.

Dani answered on the fifth ring. "This better not be about the tire. I thought we'd agreed that you'd stop following up on everything I do."

"Don't worry, sis. I'm not following up." He went on to explain why it had suddenly become urgent for her to look for the phone. "Alyssa will tell you where to look." He handed his phone to Alyssa and she gave Dani directions to the jogging trail, then returned his phone.

"Any problem heading out there now?" Cole asked.

"No," Dani replied. "If the phone is still there, I'll have it within the hour."

When he disconnected he found Alyssa staring up at him.

"This is going to sound sexist," she said, "but don't you ever worry about having your sister involved in such dangerous tasks?"

He laughed, making light of the question though it hit too close to home. "Honestly, even if I wanted to stop Dani from choosing this line of work, she wouldn't listen."

"I need your signature, Ms. Wells," the sales rep called out.

Alyssa took one last look at Cole as if she knew he wasn't telling her the whole truth and returned to the counter.

He hadn't wanted to admit it to Alyssa, but he worried about Dani all the time. More than his other siblings. She'd been through rigorous FBI training, but as a cyber crimes expert, she'd spent most of her time behind a computer and saw little action outside the office. In law enforcement, if you didn't use your skills, you lost them. Became complacent and rusty. And then when you needed those skills in life-or-death situations, they let you down. So he'd spent the past two years mentoring her and making sure she possessed the necessary tools to keep safe.

She'd proved her competence, yet he still didn't relax. Maybe it was because she was the baby of the family. Well, she *and* her twin, Derrick, but Cole knew better than to treat the Mr. Tough Guy Derrick like a baby of any sort.

"I'm ready to go," Alyssa said, her focus firmly on the phone in her hand.

Cole escorted her to the car, and by the time he climbed behind the wheel, she'd plugged her new phone into the car charger and was tapping away on her tablet. She was so busy working, she didn't even ask where they were going and he wouldn't interrupt her just to say they were headed to his rental to research cases in the area similar to Todd's murder.

Once on the road, he kept glancing at her. Her face was screwed up in concentration. He had to admit that, with the way she tilted her head, her lips curved in a smile, she made an adorable picture. Just plain adorable. She really seemed to be enjoying a task that he would pawn off on Dani in a heartbeat.

"So you like all that computer stuff, huh?" he asked, not bothering to hide his distaste.

She looked up at him. "I take it you don't."

He mocked a shudder.

"I'd have thought as an investigator you'd have to embrace all the latest technologies."

"Someone at our agency has to, but thankfully that's Dani, not me." He grinned. "I gladly hand everything over to her. I wouldn't want to deprive her of the things she likes to do most."

"Seems like she's really good at it, too."

"Top notch. And I'm not saying that just because she's my sister. She even contracts with the military to try to breach software programs before they buy from independent contractors."

"Is she married?"

Odd question. "No, why?"

"With her skills, I would imagine her spouse would feel like she was tracking him all the time." She turned her attention back to the computer. "What about you? Ever been married?" she asked offhandedly, as if she was killing time while waiting for her data to transfer to her phone.

"No."

"Ever thought about it?"

"Once, a long time ago," he said, being purposefully vague.

"Want to tell me about it?"

"No."

"Okay. I won't pry then."

Dumbfounded by her easy acquiescence, at the red light he tried to read her intent.

"What's that look for?" She laughed heartily, and he loved hearing her joy freely expressed.

"No offense to your gender, but I've never met a woman who'd let go of something like this so easily."

"Then you haven't met the right kind of woman before." Her mouth twitched with amusement, but he didn't feel at all like laughing. Just the opposite. Her easygoing personality and her ability to let go of her problems to laugh and enjoy life was attractive. Way too attractive, and he felt his interest flare.

"Clearly I haven't." They locked eyes and his pulse quickened.

She held his gaze. A dizzying current

crackled between them, making the space seem small and devoid of air. At least he couldn't seem to catch a deep breath.

From the dashboard, his phone chimed. She jumped, seeming shocked at her reaction, and he reluctantly turned away. Dani's picture popped up on the screen. He punched Talk and speaker phone.

"Dani." He paused and drew in a deep breath to calm his pulse. "You find the phone?"

"No, but the tracking software issued an alert and I know where it is."

"Where?" Alyssa asked.

"It's pinging from your duplex. Not sure which side, though. The signal isn't specific enough to tell me that."

"So Nolan has my phone and he knows I saw him last night," Alyssa shot back, fear taking over her voice.

"Or not," Cole answered calmly. "It could be in your side."

"But it wasn't there this morning. I checked everywhere."

"Just because you didn't find it doesn't mean it's not there," Dani said.

"Fine," Alyssa conceded. "For the sake of argument, say it did fall behind a sofa cushion or something like that. The phone would still be dead because no one is at my house to plug it in."

"What about the friend who watched your kids last night?" Cole asked. "Did she go home or stay over?"

"Paula? I didn't have the heart to wake her so she spent the night."

"Did she see you looking for your phone?" Dani asked. "And was she still there when you left this morning?"

"Yes."

"Then maybe she found it and plugged it in."

"If she found it she'd call to tell me—" Alyssa slapped her forehead. "I didn't have a phone for her to call."

"So this could be no big deal," Dani added. "Why don't I do a drive by of the duplex to make sure this isn't a setup? If the building is secure, the two of you can stop by and look for the phone."

"Sounds like a plan. We'll be there in five

minutes or so. Be careful, Dani." Cole checked out Alyssa to see how she was doing.

Her eyes said it all. Only time would tell if Nolan was in possession of her cell and, if so, the lengths he would go to stop her from revealing his secret life.

SIX

In her garage, Alyssa waited alone in Cole's car. He had gone inside five minutes ago to check for intruders. Dani had hurried inside the garage to wait with Alyssa before they closed the door, and now she looked out the small window, her hand resting on her weapon. She made the perfect picture for a law enforcement recruitment poster.

Alyssa, however, was a basket case. As they'd arrived, she again prayed for the ability to trust the Lord to keep them safe. But the thought of Nolan in her home and of what he might do next made her stomach churn with acid, and she regretted drinking that cup of coffee.

Cole stepped back into the garage. His focus went straight to Dani, and he gave her a clipped nod. "We're good."

Alyssa sighed out her anxiety and hopped out of the car. She joined the siblings by the door leading to her duplex. Up close, she noticed dark circles under Dani's eyes and a wary expression on Cole's face. They were sacrificing so much to help her and she couldn't be more thankful. Maybe if they went inside they would find her phone and discover Nolan wasn't after her. Then they both could relax and Dani could get some much-needed sleep.

"Can we go in?" Alyssa asked.

Cole nodded but kept his focus on Dani. "I need you to stand watch outside until we're safely on the road again."

"Got it," Dani answered, not a hint of questioning in her voice at Cole's demands.

Cole clearly expected his sister to do as told, but Alyssa still felt badly that Dani hadn't gotten any rest. She looked beat.

"Are you sure it's necessary for Dani to do this?" Alyssa asked. "She really needs to get some sleep and I hate to keep imposing."

"Hey." Dani smiled, though her face reflected her fatigue. "It's not a problem."

"But I—"

"No buts." Dani stood squarely in front of Alyssa. "This is what we're doing. End of story. No need for you to worry about us. Ever. We know our limitations. You sit back and let us do what needs to be done."

Of the same height, Alyssa looked into Dani's eyes. Her fierce determination shone through, but Alyssa still felt like she was being a burden. "I just wish I could do something for myself."

"I know," Dani said softly. "And if there's anything you can do to help, we'll let you know. Until then, let us take care of this for you. It's our job, so no more feeling bad. Okay?"

Alyssa nodded, though she still didn't like imposing this way.

"It's safest if we keep the garage door closed. I'll head out the front door." Dani squeezed Alyssa's shoulder and, with a quick look at Cole, she hurried inside.

Cole faced Alyssa, his amazing blue eyes settling on her, searching, probing, digging deep. She thought to turn away, but the concern on his face kept her locked in place. He seemed like such a good and decent man.

Trustworthy even. But could she really trust him beyond bringing Nolan to justice?

"It's hard for you to let others help you, isn't it?" he finally said.

Was it? She'd never had a problem accepting help in the past, but she did feel uncomfortable intruding on their lives.

"Given the way Saunders led you on," Cole continued, "I'm not surprised at your reluctance to let anyone get close enough to help."

Was that what she was doing? Seemed logical, she supposed. "You could be right, I guess. All I know right now is that I let Nolan into our lives. I trusted him and that makes his deceit all the harder to take." She shivered at the thought of him with the twins. "It's one thing to trample all over me, but my kids…" She shook her head. "That's not okay."

"If you think Dani and I will do anything to hurt your children, you're wrong."

"No, oh, no. That's not what I meant at all. I have nothing but respect for you and Dani and I'm so thankful God brought you both into our lives when we needed you." She met his gaze. "I guess I'm just a little short in the trust department right now."

Before he looked away, she saw the same inner turmoil she felt reflected in his eyes. He was having a hard time trusting someone, too. Maybe himself after losing the person he'd mentioned earlier.

"Cole," Dani called from inside, "I need you to lock the door after me."

"Coming," he shouted back and gestured for Alyssa to enter the duplex first.

As she passed him, he rested a hand on her shoulder. A gentle, soft touch. Nothing more. He didn't speak, didn't look at her. Just let her know he understood through a tender touch so unexpected from this powerful, often intense man that she felt a sliver of that distrust melt away.

Inside, he went directly to the small foyer that opened into their family room. Alyssa heard the lock click closed, the sound making her jump and look around the room.

How could she be this uneasy in her own home?

She spotted her phone on an old end table she'd picked up at a yard sale and refinished with bright white paint. The power cord snaked from her cell to an outlet behind the table. A small button flashed like a beacon indicating a missed call or text and pulled her across the room.

She eased through Power Rangers discarded on the floor this morning and the table holding a puzzle Paula had worked on with Brianna last night. Everything was right where they'd left it in their haste to get out of the house that morning when she took the twins to school. The house where just yesterday she'd felt comfortable and at home with the twins.

"So your phone *is* here," Cole said, coming to join her.

"I'm positive it wasn't on this table before." She picked it up and unlocked the screen. A text message alert flashed on the screen. She pressed the icon and read.

Forget what you heard last night or you die.

She gasped and dropped the phone on the sofa.

"What is it?" Cole moved closer.

She pointed at her phone. "There's a message. It's a warning."

Cole picked up her cell and then mumbled

something she couldn't make out. He held out the phone. "Do you recognize the sender's phone number?"

She forced herself to look at the screen. "No. It's not in my address book or a name would show up with the number."

"At this point, we can assume Saunders was the one who put the phone here and knows it was you last night. He likely sent this text from an untraceable phone to cover his tracks." Cole stabbed a finger at the screen. "He sent this at 10:45, so he must have found the phone just after he talked to you."

Feeling Cole watching her, she looked up at him. "But why risk bringing my cell back here? Why not wait until I got my new phone and then send a message?"

Cole's eyes darkened from a deep blue to black, ramping up her heart rate again. He opened his mouth for a moment then closed it.

Unwilling to put voice to her question again, she waited for him to speak.

"It's all about control and manipulation," he finally said and paused, his hands clenching and releasing. "Saunders wants you to know how vulnerable you are. To know that he can get to you whenever and wherever he wants. And even with us by your side, you're powerless to stop him."

The color drained from Alyssa's face, as Cole suspected it would. He hadn't wanted to answer her question, but he'd told her he'd be honest with her. He'd held true to his word, even though hearing it hurt her. And he had to accept all the blame for putting her in this position. He'd failed her. His job was to protect her and that meant not only keeping her out of Saunders's grasp, but away from the threats the creep wanted to hurl at her.

Anger over Saunders's actions and his own failures raced up his back.

"I won't let you stay here tonight," he barked out before taking the time to cool down. "Pack a bag for you and the kids. You'll stay at the beach house with Dani and me."

Alyssa took a step back and crossed her arms. He waited for her to say something, but she didn't speak. He'd come on too strong. Like earlier in the parking lot. Like he always did, and he'd made her mad. Just the opposite of what should happen. He needed her compliant and ready to act to whatever directions he gave so he could ensure her safety. Point blank, he needed her to trust him, not run from his directions.

"Look." He paused to soften his voice. "That came out all wrong. I should have recommended this option to you instead of demanding your compliance."

"You think?" she said sounding mad.

"I seem to be hitting all of your buttons today. Can I have a do-over?" He forced his lips to turn up, though he felt nothing like smiling.

His smile had no effect on her demeanor. "If this protection thing is going to work, you need to know that in addition to not being lied to, I won't be told what to do. I had enough of that with Todd."

"I'll try to be more agreeable," he said, but her body still radiated anger. "C'mon, Alyssa, I'm trying to apologize but I need you to remember my main duty is to protect you. That often means reacting at the spur of the moment and issuing directives. To keep you safe, I need to know you'll do as I say."

She seemed unimpressed with his answer. "It's not as if someone is knocking the door down right now to hurt me."

"You're right. I was out of line. I apologize."

"And I'm sorry for overreacting." She relaxed her arms but kept them crossed. "Not that it's an excuse, but Todd came home from work every day with a drill-sergeant attitude. That included grabbing my arm like you did earlier. I don't know if he didn't know how to turn it off or he didn't want to. Either way he expected us to comply with his demands."

Cole felt like a heel for bringing up these obviously painful memories. He'd known many officers who couldn't let go of the attitude they needed to stay alive on the streets, and their marriages fell apart as a result. Cole did not want to be like that, but maybe this relentless fear of failing someone was turning him into that guy.

"I'm sorry if I came off like a jerk." He took a step closer to her. "Will you and the twins stay with Dani and me?"

"As much as I've given you grief over this, I know it would be foolish to stay here," she said as a glazed look of despair spread over her face. "I'll go pack."

Grinding his jaw to relieve tension, he watched her leave the room. Seeing her defeated like this left him feeling inept and powerless. The same way he'd felt when Laura walked out on him. When Mac died. All the pain of his loss came flooding back the way it often had in the last two years.

Had he been fooling himself into thinking he could ever let go of his past to lead a normal life again? Could he ever let it go? Forget?

His phone rang, startling him.

"Dani," he answered.

"You've been in there a long time," she said. "Everything okay?"

"No." Cole filled her in on the text message. "Alyssa and her kids will be staying with us until this is all sorted."

"Good decision. It'll make our jobs easier." He was glad to hear her easy agreement confirm he hadn't overreacted for once.

"About the phone," she went on. "I'm sure Saunders would've used a throwaway to send the text, but I'll trace it to be sure."

"You want the number now?" Cole warily looked at Alyssa's phone sitting on the table.

"No. I can get it from the account info Alyssa gave me earlier. I'll run the number when we get back to the house."

"It's not likely to lead anywhere. Maybe you should catch a quick nap first."

An awkward silence filled the phone. "Dani?"

"I'm not fragile, Cole."

"I know that."

"Do you?"

"What's that supposed to mean?" he said more forcefully than he should have, but after having Alyssa question his motives he didn't have the patience for Dani to do the same thing.

"I've proved myself time and time again and you still want to coddle me."

He huffed out a sigh. "That's not what I'm doing here. You're my sister. I love you. I want what's best for you and right now that's sleep."

She didn't respond.

"C'mon, Dani. I'd say the same thing to Derrick or Ethan."

"Would you? Would you really?"

"Yeah, I would." He paused for a few seconds to make sure his next statement came out more lighthearted in hopes of alleviating the tension. "But they'd probably belt me instead of arguing with me."

"Fine," she said, sounding seriously miffed. "When we get back to the house prepare to do battle." She disconnected.

Well that was two for two. One more strike this afternoon and he was out.

As he waited for Alyssa, he wandered the family room looking at photos on bookshelves. The twins were in nearly every picture, but several of the photos included Todd and Alyssa, reflecting the good days of their marriage.

A pang of jealousy hit him. Not for the life she'd shared with Todd, but for a life he wanted. A wife. A family. But that would never happen for him.

Footsteps pounded down the stairs and Cole turned to see Alyssa laden with her belongings. She'd slung three tote bags over one shoulder and clutched a pillow and large stuffed elephant in her arms. Her eyes barely peeked over the top, but he could see enough of them to know she wasn't upset anymore.

"Let me help." He took the bags from her shoulder, catching the fresh scent of bleach from the crisp white pillowcases. "I never knew kids needed this much stuff. Or is it all for you?" he added, hoping to see the same smile he'd seen in the photos.

"Me, of course." She wrinkled her nose at him. "I especially love curling up with Ellie and Curious George." She lifted the blanket and elephant higher.

For a moment, he didn't know what to say, but she broke out laughing and he joined in, enjoying the easy camaraderie between them. He wanted more of the fun-loving, playful Alyssa. Of the woman who could make him laugh and smile with abandon. Something he hadn't been able to do or even wanted to do in a long time. She had such an incredible ability to go from dejected to carefree in a matter of minutes. How she accomplished it, he didn't know. He would ask her at some point, but right now they needed to get out of this house.

"Is this everything?" he asked.

She looked around the room and her joyful expression fell. "Should I take my old phone?"

"They could've put tracking software on it, so no." He held out his hand toward the garage, then followed her and opened the door to the backseat of his SUV. He loaded her bags then turned to her. "I hate to say this, but I'd appreciate it if you'd lie down on the floor in the back until I'm sure we're clear."

She stared at him. "Is that really necessary?"

"It's probably overkill, but—"

"—you're not taking any chances." She finished his sentence as if they'd known each other for years rather than a day. Without another word, she climbed in and he took the driver's seat.

He pressed the garage remote she'd given him and turned to look at her. "Ready?"

"As ready as I can be when I don't know what's going to happen."

He had the urge to offer comfort, but he suppressed it and slowly backed out. He checked for Dani in the rearview mirror, and when he caught her thumbs-up, he backed onto the street. She took the lead in her car and Cole trailed her. They drove through the well-manicured neighborhood, the sun beaming down on them. Small groups of children played in grassy yards and the rumble of a lawn mower hummed in the distance. Everything was as it should be, but he didn't let his guard down until they merged into heavy traffic on the main road without a tail.

"You can sit up now if you want," he called out.

"Is it okay if I sit up front with you? Riding shotgun is so much better than the backseat."

"Of course," he answered, pleased that she was willing to sit next to him after their earlier argument.

He heard her moving around and then those incredibly long legs slid through the opening between the seats, and she gracefully dropped to the passenger seat. She struggled to click her seatbelt into place and he enjoyed her cute look of concentration. He could get used to looking at her. Being with her. A relationship with her would be worth the effort of getting over his past and not letting it control him any longer.

A horn honked, and he forced his focus back to the road and his surroundings. What a fool he'd been. Letting himself be distracted when he was supposed to be vigilant and keeping watch. Didn't he learn anything from losing Mac?

Alyssa craned her neck, searching through the windows. "Where's Dani?"

"I'm giving her a chance to get ahead and check out the beach house before we arrive."

Alyssa swiveled in her seat. "Is this more overkill, like me lying on the floor?"

"Not this time. No one's been at the house in a while so it's best to check it out first."

She wrapped her arms around her waist and fell silent for the rest of the drive. When they arrived at his rental, Dani gave an all-clear signal from the open garage door. He pulled in, got out and retrieved Alyssa's belongings.

She didn't say anything and didn't look at him on the way inside. Maybe she'd gone back to thinking about their argument. Or remembering her life with Todd. That's what Cole would be doing anyway. Remembering the past.

"Can you help Alyssa choose bedrooms?"

he asked Dani in case Alyssa didn't want him hanging around while she unpacked.

"Sure," Dani said. "Give me the bags."

Cole shifted them to Dani, and Alyssa followed her through the family room and into the hallway leading to the bedrooms.

Cole went to the large window looking over the beach. A family strolled in the sun, laughing and happy. A young couple flew a kite, running with abandon. Not the kind of day he usually frequented the beach. He liked the gloomy overcast days. But he could imagine Alyssa in this crowd. She'd choose the blissful, carefree days.

A long shadow shifted in the sand by the corner of the house, catching Cole's eye. The shadow moved then disappeared. The skin on Cole's neck prickled. Someone was out there.

"Dani," he yelled and drew his weapon. "We have an intruder."

He ran for the door and heard her footfalls coming down the hallway.

"Where?" she asked, her gun in her hand.

"I saw his shadow moving around the side. Hallway's the safest place for Alyssa right now. Lock the door after me."

He stuck his head outside to evaluate the situation. All clear. He stormed outside and waited to hear the lock click closed before moving along the perimeter of the house. At the end of the building, he made another quick assessment before taking the corner.

He spotted footprints in the sand. One set heading toward him, the other away and running parallel to the building. Long strides. Big prints.

He *was* right. A man had been here.

Cole hurried along the building. He glanced through a window to confirm Alyssa wasn't in the line of fire. He checked around the back of the house. A car cranked at the road above but failed to start.

The intruder was fleeing.

With his gun in hand and arms outstretched, Cole slipped around the corner and headed up the hill. His feet sank into the sand, making it slow going. He dodged tall clumps of grasses swaying in the sea breeze. The car cranked again, caught this time and roared to life. Tires spun on sand then took hold and squealed away.

Cole closed the distance to the road and

spotted an SUV turning the corner. Not any SUV but a Pacific Bay Police cruiser. Cole got a quick look at a bald-headed man behind the wheel but couldn't make out any identifying marks on the car.

Cole jogged back to the house and made a final sweep, checking for explosive devices or other signs of tampering, before unlocking the front door.

"All clear," he yelled.

Dani eased into the family room, her weapon still in her hands. Alyssa probably thought Dani was overreacting, but Dani followed proper procedure. She kept her gun drawn until getting a visual on Cole and confirming he wasn't compromised. She turned back to the hallway. "You can come out, Alyssa."

"What'd you find?" Dani holstered her gun.

Alyssa entered the space with that worried expression he'd seen too many times in the last day lodged on her face.

Cole gestured at the sofa and waited for her to sit and for Dani to perch on the arm.

He jerked his head toward the window. "There was a man outside the house. He fled to the back and up to his vehicle at the road. It was a Pacific Bay Police car."

"Nolan?" Alyssa asked, no emotion in her voice at all. That bothered Cole more than if she'd sounded upset.

"Not unless he shaved his head since the last time we saw him." Cole kept a watchful eye on Alyssa. "Are there any bald-headed local officers?"

"Frank Gibson. The man who was talking to Nolan last night."

Dani leaned forward. "You catch any details on the car to help confirm that ID?"

"If you did," Alyssa added, "I know all of the registration numbers for the police vehicles."

Cole shook his head. "Unfortunately, he turned a corner before I could see anything. But I would appreciate having the ID numbers in case we run into another of Saunders's men."

Alyssa grabbed a notepad and pen from the table. "I'll write it all down for you."

"Thanks," Cole said, but his mind had already drifted to how he was going to increase security after this latest development. Though he'd played down the significance for Alyssa's sake, a man lurking outside the house meant only one thing to him.

If someone felt a need to watch them, then life was about to get more interesting and far more dangerous.

Before heading to the school to pick up the twins, Alyssa unpacked their bags. They'd been through so much in their young lives. The least she could do was make them feel welcome when they arrived. After putting their clothes in the long oak dresser, she placed Brianna's Curious George blanket on one of the twin beds and settled Ellie on top. Next, she pulled out an assortment of Power Rangers and displayed them on the nightstand for Riley. She stepped back to confirm the room looked like a little slice of home.

Satisfied, she returned to the family room, where she spotted Cole settled on the sofa. Leaning back, his legs casually crossed, she could picture him sitting in his own home. Maybe he'd have the TV on watching sports like Todd had often done to unwind from the job.

She waited for the uneasy feelings that usually surfaced when she thought about Todd, but for some reason only fond memories of him from the days when life had been good between them popped into her mind. Days of playing with the twins, of celebrating life's milestones and even simple things like going to the grocery store together or picking out Christmas presents for their children.

The kinder, gentler Todd was the man she wanted to remember but always had a hard time conjuring up. Maybe seeing the flashes of Cole's kindness and empathy left her longing for a man with similar characteristics in her life again.

Not a good thing.

How was she supposed to keep her defenses up around Cole if she couldn't remember how badly things had gone with Todd?

Shaking her head over her foolishness, she headed for the sofa.

Cole came to his feet and spun in one fluid motion, his eyes alert, his body ready to fight. Ah, yes. This was better. Though officially out of the law enforcement game, Cole was still a cop through and through. And cops were to be avoided at all costs if she didn't want to end up with another man who would let his job control his life.

Cole came around the sofa. "Did you get the twins' room settled?"

"Mostly."

"Let me know if there's anything you need for them to feel at home here, and I'll get it."

"Thanks," she said. "It probably seems like I'm spoiling them, but the past few years have been hard on them and I want to spare them from as much turmoil as I can."

"We'll try to make this as easy on them as possible."

"I wish I didn't have to tell them about Nolan. I don't know how they'll react if it turns out he's behind this and we have to expose him."

"No if," Cole said, his expression darkening. "Saunders is a dangerous man, and the only way out of this is to expose him."

Cole was right. There was no if. Everything pointed to Nolan being a killer, so why didn't she accept that he was the bad guy here? It's not like she was known for trusting the right men. She'd made the same mistake with Todd. Why couldn't she admit she had terrible judgment?

Cole stepped even closer, capturing her attention. "Everything will be okay, Alyssa. Trust me to know what Saunders is capable of and let me protect you from him."

She wanted to let Cole take care of everything—wanted to believe he was one of the good guys—but for all she knew a deep, dark side lingered below the surface and these flashes of kindness were simply that. Flashes.

She took a step to put distance between them before the soft expression on his face convinced her he really was a knight in shining armor. "I do trust you and Dani to take care of us, but I can't help worrying about Brianna and Riley."

"You know I won't let anything happen to them, don't you?" Cole met her gaze. She expected to see confidence there but found uncertainty instead. She guessed he was thinking about that friend he'd lost and felt responsible for. Maybe now that he seemed open, she could encourage him to share more.

"You want to talk about your friend?" she

asked, trying to sound casual. "You know, the one you alluded to in the car."

His eyebrows rose. "Where'd that come from all of a sudden?"

"You get this look on your face every time you think about him."

"This isn't really about you worrying that I can't keep you safe, is it?"

"Not at all. I just thought it would help to talk about it."

He opened his mouth but then looked at his watch. "We really should get going. I'd like to pick the kids up early from school if that's all right. It's easier to keep an eye on everything around us without other parents and children crowding around."

"Sure. Fine," Alyssa answered, but she was disappointed that he wouldn't confide in her. "I was thinking that I'd like to cook dinner tonight to repay you and Dani for your help."

"We don't need repayment."

She held up a hand. "Before you say it, I know this is your job, but I love to cook. Besides doing something nice for all of you, cooking will help keep my mind busy, too."

For a long moment he stared, his gaze almost as palpable as a physical touch. "You really are a very nice person, Alyssa Wells."

"And don't you forget that," she laughed, hiding her heavy heart over his refusal to share. "Just let me check the pantry for supplies."

He's like Todd, that nagging voice whispered in her head on her walk to the kitchen. Cold and distant when he didn't want to share his feelings. Warm and caring when he wanted to be. And it was that kindness, plus the look of interest in his eyes a moment ago, that she clearly needed to guard her heart against at all costs.

SEVEN

Cole leaned against the wall in the elementary school hallway and waited for Alyssa to emerge from the classroom with her children. The smell of paste mixed with a spaghetti lunch saturated the air. On the large art board across from him, cotton-ball clouds were glued above beaches made of real sand, making each picture different and unique. A small water fountain gurgled below.

He felt big and clumsy, so out of place in a spot where he'd once hoped he'd belong. He'd dreamed of being a father. Of everything involved in being a dad like picking up his kids from school, sitting in the drizzle of soccer matches and roughhousing on the lawn. But that dream died in Iraq. He'd tried to let go of his guilt over surviving when Mac hadn't made it. To let his family and God help. But no matter what he did, how hard he prayed, he couldn't move on.

The door opened. A boy and girl stepped into the hallway in front of Alyssa. They looked just like her. Both slender, long legs, blond hair, but the boy was taller than his sister. It was easy to see they were twins and they stuck close together. They walked slowly and carefully toward him.

After the Justices had rescued him from the foster system and made him part of their family, he'd bolted out of the classroom on early release days from school, eager to get home and play in their big yard with a rope swing. But the twins both seemed wary. Alyssa wouldn't have told them what was going on with Saunders, so maybe they were simply naturally cautious kids.

Cole pushed off the wall and waited for them to join him.

"Guys," Alyssa said when they reached him, her hand on both of their shoulders. "I'd like you to meet my friend Cole Justice."

The boy looked up at Cole then stepped in front of his sister and stuck out his hand very much resembling an adult. "Riley Wells. Pleased to meet you."

"Likewise." Cole took the small hand in his and shook, surprised at the boy's firm grip.

Riley tipped his head to the rear. "And this is my sister, Brianna. But she doesn't like to shake hands."

"Hi, Brianna." Cole smiled at the precious little girl.

She smiled shyly and stepped behind her mother.

He felt his heart melt, and for the second time in as many days, he was surprised at the intensity of his feelings.

"How do you know my mom?" Riley asked.

"I met her on the beach," Cole said, giving the answer they'd decided on during the drive to the school.

Riley's eyebrow went up and Cole could swear the kid was more grown up than many adults he'd met. Before Riley could probe deeper, Cole gestured toward the exit. "We should get going if we're going to stop at the grocery store on the way home."

The trio set off, and thinking about Riley, Cole followed. The boy reminded Cole of

Derrick when he and Dani joined the Justice family. Nearly ten when their parents died in an auto accident, Derrick thought he had to take care of Dani. He still did. Sticking up for her and protecting her, but now Dani balked at his overprotectiveness in the same way she did with Cole.

At the front door of the school, Cole stepped in front of them and made a quick sweep of the parking lot. He tried to act casual, but Riley watched his every move and suspicion lighted on his face. Maybe this wasn't about Cole. Maybe he was suspicious all the time. Losing a parent could cause that kind of behavior. So could living with a mother who was a drug addict and being shuffled from foster family to foster family. Cole knew that firsthand.

He opened the door and moved them quickly to his car. Once on the road, he listened to Alyssa share her expectations of them while staying with him. She reminded him of his adoptive mom, who'd often done the same thing with them on family outings. How he missed his adoptive parents. Life would be different if they were here. For one thing, they wouldn't put up with the two-year funk he'd been going through.

Had he been dishonoring their memory and everything they'd done for him by not trying harder to get over Iraq?

He drove into the grocery store lot and returned his attention to ensuring the little family's safety. Their stop for groceries was quick and uneventful, and they soon neared the rental house driveway.

"Wow," Riley said staring at the house. "You must be rich."

Cole chuckled and Alyssa frowned. "That's exactly the kind of thing I don't want you to say, Riley."

"Don't know why not. It's not a bad thing to be rich, is it?"

"No, but it's not something people talk about."

"Why not?"

"Because they don't."

Riley's eyebrows drew together. "I don't get grown-ups sometimes. If we had a house like this, I wouldn't care if anyone said we were rich."

"I don't care, either, Riley," Cole said easing past another Justice Agency vehicle in the driveway. "But this isn't my house. I'm renting it."

"Oh." He sounded so let down that Cole wished he did own this house and the kid didn't have to be disappointed in yet another thing.

Wondering which siblings' car sat in the drive, Cole opened the back door of his vehicle for the twins. Riley jumped down, his backpack already settled on his back. Brianna looked afraid of the height and Cole offered his hand. She slipped her fingers in his, her hand so tiny in his palm that it gave him a moment's pause as he helped her down. Brianna kept hold of his hand, even after she reached the ground.

Alyssa watched them, her careful motherly look in place as if she didn't trust him with her child. And why would she? Especially after Saunders inflicted his damage on her emotions. She didn't know enough about Cole to know he'd never harm a child.

"I need to get the groceries," he said to Brianna, expecting she'd let go, but she clung to his hand.

"I can carry them." Riley snagged the heavy bags, pulling down his shoulders, but he held up under the weight and trudged toward the door.

"Let me take one of those bags," Alyssa offered.

Riley stepped out of reach. "I can do it, Mom."

She followed her son inside, and Cole brought up the rear with Brianna. He looked at her hand in his. Listened to her little footsteps tapping on the concrete in an effort to keep up with his bigger stride, and his heart constricted over all he was missing in life. All the things his parents had wanted for him.

Inside the family room, Riley pointed at Dani standing next to their surprise visitor, Derrick. "Look, Bri. They're just like us."

Brianna broke away, joining Riley.

"Derrick." Cole watched his little brother carefully to determine the reason for his visit. "I didn't expect you."

"Couldn't wait to see my favorite brother." Derrick came across the room and gave Cole a good-natured punch to the shoulder.

"My brother, Derrick," Cole said to Alyssa.

"And I'm guessing Dani's twin, as my son aptly pointed out." While taking the grocery bags from Riley, Alyssa introduced her kids to Derrick and Dani.

"Always good to meet fellow twins." Derrick ruffled Riley's hair.

Riley took a step back and stuck out his hand to shake. Derrick seemed puzzled by Riley's behavior but recovered quickly and clasped Riley's hand then moved to Alyssa and did the same thing.

After the handshake she lifted one of the bags. "I bought some food for the kids' afternoon snack. Would it be okay if they sat at the counter to eat?"

"Sure," Dani said.

"And can they use the bathroom to wash up first?"

Dani nodded. "C'mon, guys. I'll show you where it is."

Alyssa went into the kitchen and Dani led the way to the bathroom.

Once they were out of earshot, Cole turned to Derrick. "I'm glad you're here. When the kids are settled I'd like to talk to you about an idea I have to end this thing with Saunders."

"Why wait?" Derrick asked.

"Alyssa needs to be included in this conversation and it's not something we should talk about in front of the twins." Cole glanced at her in the kitchen and saw the tight pinch of her mouth. Cole didn't want to burden her with details, but this involved her. No, that wasn't right. This didn't just involve her. It was all about her. No matter how much it hurt to talk about Saunders, Cole wasn't about to exclude her from a life-and-death decision.

Alyssa set a plate of cheese and crackers on the counter in front of the twins. The room sizzled with tension, but thankfully, the twins were unaware. When Alyssa and Dani made eye contact, Dani gave her a comforting smile. A smile that said Derrick had already told his sister about the secretive discussion he'd had with Cole earlier. After several of those smiles, Dani moved closer. "Why don't I stay here while you talk with Cole and Derrick?" Dani didn't wait for agreement but grabbed a cracker and leaned on the counter in front of the twins. "So you two are like in high school, right?"

Brianna giggled while Riley rolled his eyes. "Try first grade."

"Guess I was way off then." Dani shoved the cracker in her mouth and shooed Alyssa out of the room.

She went into the family room and found the brothers seated in chairs facing the ocean. Derrick not only looked like Dani with his blond hair and eyes the color of roasted coffee beans, but his expressions were the same, too. As the mother of twins, she knew he must possess unique mannerisms, but right now she could only see the similarities. The one thing he had in common with Cole was his rigid body language and a wary expression darkened his face when he looked up and saw her coming his way. They both quit talking, and she hoped Cole wasn't going behind her back and had decided to keep her out of the loop.

"May I join you?" she asked, trying to play down her unease.

Cole patted the cushion next to him "That would be good. We need to talk."

Alyssa ignored the rising tension and sat on the plush sofa.

Cole stretched his arm along the back of the sofa. "I asked Derrick to do a background check on Saunders and other key players."

"By other key players you mean who exactly?" She leaned forward in anticipation of the answer.

"Your former husband and you," Cole answered matter-of-factly, keeping his focus on her.

She felt Derrick watching her, too, so she met his inquisitive gaze. "And I take it by your expression that you found something troubling."

Derrick stretched out his long legs, looking at ease, but she could see the same tension that gripped Cole. "Cole asked me to start with Saunders and I did. I located an old friend of his who'd moved to Portland and is now doing time for narcotics distribution. Prison records show he's still in contact with Saunders via the phone."

"And who is this friend?" Alyssa asked.

"John Wilmer. Ring any bells?"

She thought about friends she'd seen with Nolan, but couldn't come up with a John Wilmer. She shook her head. "I know there are Wilmers living in Pacific Bay, but I've never heard of a John."

"With his incarceration, his family probably doesn't talk about him," Cole offered. "We're thinking he got Saunders involved in the drug game."

"And we also think the only way Saunders has escaped the same incarceration as Wilmer is because he's a police officer and the police chief's son," Derrick added.

"So it looks like Nolan really is dealing drugs and getting away with it, then," Alyssa said, trying to ignore the sinking feeling in the pit of her stomach.

Cole's concerned expression said she hadn't managed it. He reached out a hand as if he was going to take hers to offer his support, but then he glanced at his brother and dropped his arm to his side. "If we try to take Saunders down, his department will likely close ranks. We'll need to involve outside law enforcement if we're to get him off the street. Even then, his fellow officers could make life difficult for us by covering for him."

Alyssa swallowed hard. "As much as I hate to admit it, I think you're right. I've known

Chief Saunders for years. He dotes on Nolan and would do everything he could to protect his son."

"Even if it was illegal?" Derrick asked.

"Yeah, even then." She sighed and wondered how on Earth they were going to stop Nolan.

"Then let me share an idea I have." Cole scooted closer to her. She could feel the warmth from his body, giving her a measure of comfort. "I believe our key to bringing Saunders to justice is to try to turn one of his men against him. Since Frank Gibson expressed interest in getting out of the group last night, he's our best candidate. Can you tell me anything about him that might help us succeed with him?"

Alyssa chewed on her lip and considered what she knew about Frank that could help. "He's all about family. Last night he said he was feeling guilty and begged Nolan to let him off their team. He said he'd only joined up because he needed money to pay for his son's leukemia treatments."

"And what is his son's status now?" Derrick asked.

"He's in remission, thankfully. Frank said last night that their bills were all caught up and they don't need the extra money anymore."

"Then it's time I pay Gibson a visit," Cole said forcefully. "Hopefully I can persuade him that turning on Saunders is in his and his family's best interest."

Cole's words settled in and Alyssa felt a chill run through her body. "You're not going alone, are you?"

He gave a solemn nod.

Her stomach clamped down on the cheese she'd just consumed. She made eye contact with Cole and hoped it transmitted her worry for his safety. "Won't that be dangerous?"

"Not likely," he answered.

Derrick snorted, and Alyssa snapped her head in his direction. His look contradicted Cole's denial.

"You can't let Cole go alone," Alyssa pleaded with Derrick.

Derrick watched his older brother for a minute. "Maybe Alyssa's right, and I should tag along, bro. Just to be safe."

Cole shook his head. "It's more important for you to stay here to help Dani."

Derrick's eyebrows went up. "I'll stay if that's what you want, but I'm not sure it's the best move."

"It's what I want," Cole said firmly, then met Alyssa's eyes for a long, lingering look. "If I'm going to be out of the house, Derrick will be needed here. Your safety comes first."

Alyssa appreciated Cole thinking of them first, but after Nolan's betrayal, she knew people were unpredictable and dangerous. When pushed to the wall, even those closest to her could commit murder. And right now, she feared that included Frank Gibson.

EIGHT

Cole turned into Alyssa's neighborhood. She'd surprised him when she'd said Gibson lived in her subdivision. Apparently so did several other officers on the force. This reasonably priced neighborhood was one of the few in an area where most properties were out of reach of the working class.

Nearing her duplex, Cole spotted a police SUV in her driveway. He came to a stop and dug out the list of vehicle numbers Alyssa provided earlier. He checked the list then looked at the car to confirm.

What was Gibson doing at Alyssa's house?

Only one way to find out.

Cole pulled to the curb and eased out of his SUV. He quietly approached the house and tried the doorknob. Unlocked.

Was Gibson's car parked out front to lure

Cole or Alyssa into the home? If so, he wouldn't fall for it. He silently released the knob and crept to the back door leading onto a small deck. The lack of window coverings on the sliding patio door allowed him a clear view inside the house.

A bald-headed man wearing a cop's uniform sat at the small dining table, confirming the man's identity as Officer Gibson. His back to Cole, he'd drawn his gun and had it fixed on the front door. If Cole had opened that door, Gibson could've plugged him. Even wearing his vest, Cole could've been killed. But Cole didn't think Gibson was here for him. More likely he was lying in wait for Alyssa.

The thought of Gibson anywhere near Alyssa sent rage barreling through his chest. He hurried to the side door of the garage. With lock-picking tools, he was inside in under a minute. Drawing his gun, he padded down a short hallway and crept up behind Gibson.

He pressed his weapon into the man's neck. "Set your gun on the table. Nice and easy now."

Cole ground his gun deeper and Gibson moved slowly. Once he'd set his service weapon on the table, Cole shoved it in his belt.

Keeping his gun trained on Gibson, Cole stepped in front of him "Well, well, well, Officer Gibson. Care to tell me what you're doing in Alyssa's house?"

Gibson didn't say a word, but Cole saw his gaze move around the room, looking for a way out, as any good cop would in this situation.

Cole took a step closer. "I see Saunders has you doing his dirty work again. Too bad you're the one who'll take a fall for him."

"I have a key to the property given to me by the owner so you don't have anything on me." He crossed his arms and looked at the floor.

On the off chance they didn't know that Alyssa was the one they'd been chasing on the beach, Cole couldn't admit to Alyssa overhearing their meeting or he'd implicate her. So he'd go on a fishing expedition and see what he could turn up on Todd Wells's murder instead.

"But we do have something on you, Gibson. And that means when we finalize our investigation you'll be doing time right along with Saunders for the death of Todd Wells."

Gibson's head shot up. "I didn't have anything to do with that."

"But you know who did and since you're in business with him, you'll be hard-pressed to prove you weren't involved," Cole said, baiting the man in hopes of getting him to turn on Saunders. "At the very least you're going away for the meth distribution."

Gibson scoffed. "No one on the force is going to arrest me."

"True, but lucky for me I have contacts in other agencies. They'll be only too happy to haul you in."

Gibson raised a challenging eyebrow. "You don't have any credible evidence. If you did, I'd already be sitting in a six-by-eight."

He was right. He would be sitting in jail, but Cole wouldn't let him know that. "Don't I? Or am I simply waiting until I've gathered enough evidence to bring down the whole operation?"

Gibson's bravado wavered and Cole went in to close the deal. "I'm sure we can work out a deal for you if you tell us what you know about Wells's death and agree to testify."

Gibson pondered for a few moments. "I didn't see him do it."

"But you know where we might find the evidence to convict him, don't you?"

"Yes."

"That'll do."

Gibson ran a hand over his head now slick with sweat. "Let's be clear here. I won't do anything to put my family in danger."

"I get that, but Saunders is going down for this murder and distributing meth whether you testify or not. Help us and save yourself, or go down with him."

Gibson didn't seem inclined to roll over on Saunders so Cole started backing toward the door. "It might help you make the right decision if you remember what they do to cops in prison."

"Wait," Gibson called out. "I'll do it. *If* I get complete immunity on all charges."

"I can't promise that."

"Then you don't have a deal until you can."

"I'll have to check with my contacts."

"You do that and when you can give me

immunity in writing, I'll give you Wells's killer."

Partial compliance was not exactly how Cole hoped this would go down, but it was progress. "And now you can tell me what you're doing here."

"I'm supposed to detain Alyssa if she comes home."

"And then?"

"He plans to eliminate her."

An uneasy feeling settled in Cole's gut. He needed to get out of here. His brother and sister were good at their jobs, but he wouldn't relax until Alyssa was under his supervision again. He jerked his gun at the door. "I'll escort you out."

Gibson got up and, not taking his eyes off Cole, backed to the door.

Cole stopped a few feet away and holstered his weapon. He didn't want to leave himself unprotected, but he needed to give Gibson's gun back to him. It wouldn't do for Gibson to report the loss of his service weapon and raise Saunders's suspicions.

Cole cleared the chamber, withdrew the ammo clip and drew his gun again before joining Gibson at the door. "If I catch you anywhere near Alyssa Wells or her children, I not only won't get you that deal, but I'll also make sure you get the full penalty due. Got that?"

Gibson nodded and grabbed his gun then backed outside.

After Gibson drove off, Cole turned the lock on the doorknob and hurried to his vehicle. He felt confident he'd find a law enforcement agency to cut Gibson a deal on the charges. It wasn't every day an opportunity arose to arrest the boss of a drug operation and take a killer off the street at the same time. Cole only hoped they could act before Saunders sent another man after Alyssa. A man Cole might not be able to reason with and who would do his best to take her life.

With dinner in the oven, Alyssa needed something to do to keep from worrying about Cole's visit to Frank. She'd often felt unsettled when Todd was a police officer, wondering if he would make it through the day, but that was because she loved Todd. She'd admit she was attracted to Cole, but she certainly wasn't in love with him.

She didn't even trust him, so why had she been so troubled since he'd walked out the door? And why couldn't she quit thinking about all the things that could go wrong in his meeting with Frank?

With a groan, she marched down the hall to check on Riley and Brianna. They sat on the floor of their bedroom playing a Curious George matching game. Riley's face bore the serious look that had rarely left his young face since Todd died.

What was going to happen when, if everything went according to plan, he also lost Nolan, who was almost like a father to him? Both men her son had admired and wanted to emulate had let him down. Fortunately, she didn't have to let him or Brianna know about Nolan until he was arrested for his crimes. If she shared anything sooner, not only might she share wrong information, confusing her children, but they could inadvertently let something about Nolan slip at school. With Pacific Bay being such a small town, Nolan could hear about it and flee. There was no

way she'd risk letting him get away with killing Todd.

"Mom," Brianna's sweet voice called out,
"can we go home?"

Alyssa would like nothing more than to
scoop her children into her arms and take
them home, but Nolan might be there and she
couldn't risk it. "Our friends have invited us
to stay the night. We can pretend it's a big
adventure."

"But my TV show is on and I'm missing
it." Brianna's whine grated on Alyssa's already raw nerves.

"Come on, Bri," Riley said. "One night isn't
gonna kill you."

She bent down and kissed the top of her
daughter's head. "He's right, sweetie."

"'Sides," Riley added, "you're winning
right now so I'm the one who should be whin-
ing—not you."

Brianna's eyes perked up and she snapped
down another card. "Match."

Satisfied a crisis had been averted, Alyssa
went back to the family room. The mouth-
watering scent of an onion-topped roast she'd

prepared drifted from the kitchen. Despite her concern for Cole, her stomach grumbled.

Dani and Derrick sat at the kitchen island, both working on computers. Alyssa didn't want to interrupt them, but she couldn't sit idly by and wait for news of Cole, so she paced the floor in the family room.

"You need to stay away from the windows, Alyssa," Dani called out.

"Sorry." Alyssa gave Dani an apologetic look. "I just can't seem to sit still."

Dani climbed off her stool. "It's understandable. You're worried about what Saunders has planned."

She nodded and evaded a more detailed answer by walking away. She went to a floor-to-ceiling bookcase loaded with novels and picked up a large seashell.

"Is there something else bothering you?" Dani asked.

How could Alyssa answer that? She couldn't. Not without admitting she was worried for Cole, making her think she was coming to care for him.

"Alyssa." Dani's voice came from right behind her, and Alyssa jumped, nearly dropping the shell. "Sorry to scare you like that."

Alyssa put the shell back. "I'm just a little jumpy."

"It's probably none of my business, but is this about Cole?" Dani's gaze burrowed into Alyssa.

Not willing to talk about Cole, Alyssa shrugged.

"I thought so." Dani smiled knowingly. "I see the way you look at him when you think no one is watching."

Had she really been that transparent with her feelings?

A car door slammed outside. Dani spun toward the door, her hand automatically going for her weapon.

"Thank goodness." Eager to find out what had happened with Frank, Alyssa started across the room.

"Don't open the door. It might not be Cole." Dani rushed ahead of Alyssa.

Alyssa thought Dani was overreacting, but she knew this family was all about protecting her. She stood back and waited while Dani peeked through the blinds covering a side window.

"Is it Cole?" Alyssa asked.

"Yes."

Alyssa took several deep breaths and hissed out her anxiety, surprising herself at how much she'd let thoughts of Cole putting himself in danger get to her.

Dani pulled open the door and Cole stepped inside. His usual focused expression—eyes narrowed, jaw firm—said he had something on his mind, but he didn't look worried or agitated.

"What happened? Did Frank agree? Will we be able to have Nolan arrested?" The words flew out of Alyssa's mouth as if she were a child on Christmas morning thrilled with her presents.

Dani laughed. "Alyssa's been worried about you. She'd been jittery and pacing the floor waiting for you to get back."

Cole arched a brow and studied Alyssa. She blushed under his careful scrutiny and he smiled, so soft, so sweet, so intimate, that she nearly forgot to breathe.

"So what happened with Gibson?" Dani asked, abruptly ending their moment.

"Why don't we sit down?" Cole's voice sounded as unsteady as Alyssa's legs felt. "Care to join us, Derrick?"

"Thought you'd never ask." Derrick jumped off his stool.

Alyssa crossed the room and dropped onto the sofa. Cole took a seat next to her. Dani and Derrick sat in plump chairs on the other side of a large coffee table. Alyssa didn't need Cole sitting this close right now and wished he'd chosen the other side of the table. She scooted back until she couldn't move another inch, which earned her another arch of his brow.

"Well?" she asked, taking the focus off her discomfort.

"I found Gibson. At your house."

"My house? But why? And how?"

"Saunders gave him a key to wait for you. He was ordered to detain you if you came home."

"And then what?" Her fear built in anticipation of his answer.

"That's not important right now. What we

need to focus on is that he claims to have evidence to implicate Saunders in Todd's murder."

"And you believe him?" Derrick asked, sounding skeptical.

"As much as one can believe a dirty cop."

Dani studied her older brother for long moments, making Alyssa wonder what was going through her mind.

"What if Gibson's playing you?" she finally asked.

"Worst case scenario is he tells Saunders we're on to him." Cole's expression hardened into solid granite. "Something Saunders already knows."

"Do you think this might be enough to keep Nolan from coming after me?" Alyssa imbued her voice with the urgency she felt.

"Not likely." Cole met her gaze and the intensity burning in his eyes reminded her of another night when she'd faced physical danger. The night Todd had hit her.

A shiver claimed her body, but she forced herself to remember that she wasn't alone tonight. She had the amazing Justice family at her side. "If Nolan knows about all of you, then he has to know the odds of getting to me are against him."

"He's a cop," Cole said, his voice filled with resignation. "At times we all think we're invincible and we charge in where we shouldn't."

Alyssa had seen that very thing in men on the force, and that was part of the reason she used to worry for Todd. He didn't know when to pull back from danger. Was Cole the same? Reckless when it came to his safety? Would he do something foolish to put himself in harm's way? She couldn't stand it if he got hurt. "If what you're saying is true, Nolan will still try to come after me, and that means everyone here is in danger."

Cole shrugged off her comment. "At the very least he'll try to find out if we have any evidence against him. So it's key that we resolve this as soon as possible. Until then, we'll keep you under wraps, and we'll all be fine." Cole focused on Dani. "Gibson expects immunity on the drug trafficking charges in exchange for his testimony. Can you contact the DEA to see if they'll play ball?"

"I'll do it right now." She got up.

"And I'll need you to find all the information you can on Gibson. Track his phone, et cetera. Okay?"

"I'll start with the DEA and then get to work on Gibson." She pulled her phone from her pocket and went down the hallway.

"Could this all be over if the DEA agrees to Frank's terms?" Alyssa clutched her hands as she waited for Cole's reaction.

Tension radiated off him in rolling waves. "Could be, but there are still too many variables to let our guard down yet."

The weight of her tumultuous situation settled on her shoulders. She still hated to believe Nolan would try to harm her, but then again, he'd killed Todd and she couldn't have believed that would happen, either.

How could she ever have trusted him?

Her skin started to crawl, and she couldn't sit still. She got up and resumed her pacing. She heard Cole rise and when she turned to head back across the room he stood in her path.

"You're too close to the windows," he said softly, as if he understood everything going through her mind and didn't want to intrude but needed to keep her safe.

She looked up at him and for the first time she really understood the law enforcement mentality. Police officers were strong protectors and they always wanted to be ready to help. That's why so many of them carried weapons when off duty. Even being married to an officer for nine years, she hadn't really felt the weight of the burden they bore until this dangerous situation invaded her life.

She glanced at the black wall of windows Cole had warned her away from. He'd been right when he'd said they were hard to defend against. "Guess you're wishing you'd rented a house with fewer windows."

"I have to admit it would be easier," he said with steel in his voice. "But I'm not going to let these windows stop me. I'll do everything within my power to protect you, even if it means giving up my life."

She knew he spoke the truth, and she feared that before all of this was over, he would have to choose between protecting her and putting his life on the line.

NINE

Yawning from a fitful night's sleep, Cole sipped his last cup of coffee before starting his day. He sat next to Dani and Derrick at the large dining table while Alyssa struggled to get the twins ready so Dani could drive them to school. How hard it must be to be a single parent. So hard that Cole felt guilty when he let a laugh escape over Riley and Brianna's antics, drawing Alyssa's attention. She was clearly frustrated, but she didn't show it to the children.

Cole was coming to see that she was a wonderful mother. Though she'd found herself staying in a stranger's home, she'd insisted on keeping the twins' lives as close to normal as possible. And that included a short devotion with them after breakfast. Cole had listened carefully to the message about letting

God take charge of their lives, and he could almost believe turning his problems over to God again was the answer he sought to all of his troubles.

Almost.

"Kids, get your backpacks from the bedroom," Alyssa said in her mom tone.

Cole could see Riley start to role his eyes then stop and head down the hall. Brianna followed him out of the room.

"I'm sorry it's taking so long to get them ready," Alyssa said coming over to the table.

Dani waved a hand. "No problem."

Alyssa blew a strand of hair out of her face and settled her hands on her hips. "We're not usually this disorganized."

"Don't sweat it," Derrick said. "If you'd seen Mom trying to get all five of us out of the house when we were growing up, you'd realize this is nothing."

Alyssa smiled at Derrick. The way her face lit up gave Cole a moment of jealousy. He wanted to be the one to make her smile with so much joy.

Dani's phone vibrated on the table, and she glanced at it. "It's Agent Carter at the DEA."

She lifted it to her ear. "Tell me you have good news, Carter," she said then listened intently. "So you're willing to meet with us?"

The twins came back into the room, and Cole slashed a hand across his throat to stop Dani from saying anything to scare them. She nodded her acknowledgment and left the room to finish her conversation, but Riley had already noticed Alyssa's tension.

Cole didn't want the little guy to worry so Cole said the first thing that came to his mind. "Dani isn't quite ready to go. This place has a ton of games. How about we choose one to play after school?" He took them to a tall cabinet on the back wall.

"Whoa!" Riley's eyes went wide. "There are, like, a bazillion games here."

Brianna went straight to Pretty Pretty Princess and pulled it out. "I want to play this one."

"That one's for sissies," Riley said.

Cole agreed with Riley—not that it was for sissies, but a game that involved putting on jewelry and a crown appealed more to girls. But when Brianna scrunched up her face, Cole didn't have the heart to voice his agreement with Riley.

"You'll have time to play more than one game," he said to Riley. "Each of you can choose one."

Brianna's lips split in a grin, revealing a gap where a new tooth was emerging. She hugged the game to her chest.

"I want this one." Riley pulled out Monopoly Junior. "Do I really have to play Pretty Pretty Princess?"

"What do you think?"

"My mom's gonna say if I want to play my game then I have to play Brianna's, too."

"I guess that answers your question then." He ruffled Riley's hair.

He frowned. "I was kinda hoping since we were at your house we could use your rules."

"My rule would be the same as your mom's." Cole slung an arm around Riley's shoulder and guided him toward the door.

Brianna came closer and walked beside him, slipping her hand into his.

Her soft touch melted another chunk of the ice around his heart, and he didn't know how to handle it. This thawing of his soul was still so new, so fresh, that the way it made him feel scared him as much as thoughts of Saunders ever could.

Shocked at Brianna's continued fondness for Cole, Alyssa joined Dani in the kitchen as she finished her conversation with Carter. Alyssa grabbed lunch bags, her mind on the change in Brianna. Her daughter never trusted people she didn't know. Especially not men. So why was she willing to trust Cole?

Alyssa glanced through the large opening into the family room. Cole helped the kids into jackets, joking and laughing with them like he hadn't a care in the world.

Is this You, God? Trying to get me to see he's as good a man as he seems to be?

"He looks happy, doesn't he?" Dani disconnected and shoved her phone into her jeans pocket.

"You mean Cole?" Alyssa clarified.

"Yeah. I haven't seen him smile like that in years. You and your family are good for him."

Alyssa still wasn't ready to talk about Cole so she went to the refrigerator and grabbed juice boxes and cheese sticks.

When she turned, Dani was waiting. "You do care about him, don't you?"

Alyssa set the lunch supplies on the counter. "Yes, of course. He's been so helpful and kind. And I can never repay him or all of you for risking your lives for us."

Dani's chin when up. "That's not what I meant and you know it."

Unwilling to have this discussion with Dani, Alyssa ignored the comment and put peanut butter and jelly sandwiches in a bag then added juice boxes and cheese sticks.

"He's an amazing guy, Alyssa. Any woman would be lucky to have him." Dani gave Alyssa a long look then headed into the living room.

Alyssa wrote the twins' names on the bags then watched Dani and Cole. They were so protective of each other. Derrick was probably the same way. How great it would be to have a big family. An only child, Alyssa had always wanted siblings. She was thrilled the day she learned she was expecting twins. Though they'd had a tough life, they also had a special bond to help them get through life's trials.

Cole looked up and caught her studying him. He crossed over to her and smiled that kind of sleepy, charming little grin he'd greeted her with this morning and her pulse thrummed. "Dani's ready to take the twins to school if you want to say goodbye."

She peered at her children and a sudden fear clutched her heart. "Are you sure they'll be okay? I mean, I trust Dani, I really do, but it'd be better if you took them."

"I'm not leaving you, Alyssa." Gone was the warmth, his lethal tone taking over. "Dani will stay at the school all day. She's very capable."

"But you're better. Admit it."

"I'm more than willing to admit it." He paused and smiled wryly. "But the threat is to you, not the twins, and I need to stay where the threat is greatest."

He had a point, and she knew she needed his protection.

"You said yourself that you don't think Saunders would hurt the kids," Cole went on as if he thought she would continue to argue with him.

"I don't, but then he's done many things I didn't think he was capable of doing."

"If you really think they're in danger, we could keep them home. But honestly, if Saunders comes for you today, it would be better if they were in school."

"You're right. I'll say goodbye to them." She picked up their lunch bags and headed for the living room, praying on the way that her children and Dani wouldn't run into any harm today.

Late that afternoon, Cole leaned back from his computer and stretched his arms overhead. Across the table, Alyssa bent over Brianna, helping her with spelling homework. Riley was sitting next to his sister and writing with a thick pencil. The scene was so cozy it was hard to believe Agent Carter from the DEA had sat at the same table this morning and promised to secure a deal for Gibson.

Riley suddenly looked up at Cole. "How come you have to do homework at your age?"

Cole stifled a laugh. "I'm not doing homework. I'm just working."

"But you're home and you're working so why isn't it homework?"

Alyssa studied her son. "Do you really want an answer to that, or are you putting off doing your spelling?"

His face took on a sheepish look.

"That's what I thought. Now back to the spelling." Alyssa looked down. Cole caught her gaze and they shared a smile. Being part of this private moment made him feel like a member of her family, and a longing for what he couldn't have was a physical ache.

What was it about this woman that she could make this kind of impact on him?

Brianna asked a question and Alyssa changed her focus to her daughter. He went back to his research and focused on another news story about an unsolved murder in the area. He searched the article, looking for a similar pattern to Todd's murder. Earlier in the afternoon, he and Alyssa had found two comparable cases and he'd phoned the local police departments to secure additional information. The chiefs all promised to email details of their cases. So far, he'd heard nothing.

He scrolled down the *Daily Astorian*'s Web

site. A man's body had been found in the landfill with meth in his bloodstream. He was a known drug dealer, and local authorities believed his death was related to his occupation. As of the date of the story, the case hadn't been solved.

The police chief in Astoria was an old family friend so Cole fired off an email asking for additional information about the case. He went back to his search, but an hour or so later when a spicy aroma drifted into the room and made his mouth water, he couldn't concentrate any longer.

"How long until dinner?" he asked Alyssa.

She glanced at the clock above the fireplace. "If these two little monsters will wash up while you find Dani and Derrick, I'll have the chili on the table when you come back. Deal?" She smiled widely.

"Deal." He smiled back at her, that goofy feeling in his stomach again.

He hurried to corral everyone at the table and, as promised, Alyssa had steaming bowls of chili and thick corn bread on a plate with a dish of honey butter waiting to melt onto the perfectly browned tops.

As they ate, Dani and Derrick kept the conversation going by entertaining everyone with stories of growing up as twins.

"Enough," Alyssa said, nodding at her twins. "Don't give these two any more ideas of what they can get away with when they get older."

"Aw, Mom, it was fun," Brianna grumbled.

Alyssa stood and placed her hands on the twins' shoulders. "It's bath time for the two of you. If you make it quick, I'll read to you before bed."

Brianna and Riley got up without a comment or even a look and headed toward the bathroom. Alyssa started picking up dishes.

Dani held up her hand. "You and Cole have been working hard all day. Derrick and I'll do the dishes while you two relax in the family room."

"Speak for yourself, sis." Derrick stood and yawned. "I'm gonna catch some sleep before I stand watch out here all night."

"Fine," Dani said. "I can handle the dishes by myself. You two get out of here." She made a shooing motion with her hands.

Cole saw right through Dani's ploy to get

him together with Alyssa. But if Alyssa noticed, she didn't say a word. Cole wasn't about to encourage the relationship his sister hoped for. He opened his mouth to offer an excuse when his phone rang.

"Agent Carter," Cole, thankful for the interruption, said into his phone.

"I need to talk to you," Carter barked. "In person."

"That doesn't sound good."

"Just a precaution. With the way phones are hacked these days I don't want to take a chance of someone overhearing us."

Cole knew the Justice cells were secure. Dani made sure of that, but he couldn't vouch for Carter's phone. "Can you come to the house?"

"I can be there in five minutes."

"I'll wait for you on the deck." Cole disconnected and stowed his phone. "Carter's coming over to talk."

Worry consumed Alyssa's face, and the desire to comfort her nearly outweighed Cole's common sense to keep her at arm's length. He had to get out of here. "I'll wait for him on the deck so the twins don't accidently hear our conversation." He went to retrieve his jacket.

"Did he say what this is about?" Alyssa called after him.

"No." He shrugged into his jacket.

"It can't be good news if he wants to see you in person."

"It's just a precaution." He fisted his hands to keep from reaching out and smoothing the worry lines in her forehead or holding her to take away the fear lurking in her eyes.

"Don't worry, Alyssa. You're safe." Dani shot Cole a harsh look. "We won't let anything happen to any of you."

"Thanks," Alyssa said, not looking at Cole. "I'll go help the twins."

The minute Alyssa disappeared down the hallway, Dani jabbed him in the arm. "What was that all about?"

"Ouch," he complained.

"You deserved it. She was afraid and you made it worse. And don't tell me you didn't see it. When it comes to Alyssa you don't miss a thing."

He didn't want to get into this discussion with Dani. "I'll be on the deck."

"So you're going to run from this just like you're running from what happened in Iraq?" she called after him.

He cringed at her tone but kept going and stepped into an icy-cold wind. The temperature had plummeted since sundown, and with the deck raised high above ground to catch the view, ice formed quickly.

He leaned on the railing and stared into the starless night. Cold seeped through his coat and bit into his skin. Good. He deserved to be as cold on the outside as he felt on the inside. He wanted to let go of all his issues and embrace these feelings for Alyssa, embrace the desire to find a wife and have a family, but he'd been frozen for so many years that thawing wasn't as simple as everyone made it out to be.

After a while, he felt movement behind him and turned in time to witness the cozy scene inside. Alyssa had the twins fresh from their baths tucked under her arms and they settled onto the sofa to read that promised bedtime story. They appeared to be the ideal little family. Except he knew they had issues like every family had. And he had no right to add to that turmoil by falling for Alyssa and saddling her with his problems.

Soft footfalls climbing the steps changed his focus. Carter, his moves measured and deliberate in the dark, joined him.

"Justice." Carter tipped his head at the house. "Sorry about pulling you away from the family. It'd be a lot nicer inside than waiting out here for me."

"No problem," Cole answered. "So what do you have?"

"I've been trying to locate Gibson, but he's missing."

"You're sure?"

He nodded. "He's not at his home. His wife says he's at work, but he's not there. I've been hounding them down at the police station all day. Finally got an employee to tell me he called in last night saying he was taking a few days off. They haven't heard from him since."

"We both know he's not taking a few days off."

"Agreed, but I don't have anything concrete to use for a warrant for his home or his phone, so there's nothing I can do about it."

"I anticipated this thing with Gibson going

south. Dani's already working on obtaining Gibson's phone records."

Carter shook his head. "Sometimes I wish I was on your side of the fence. It'd be a whole lot easier to get what I need without the law constraining my moves."

"It has its good points at times, but we have to work harder for information that you have at your fingertips. I figure it's a wash."

"Point taken." Carter gestured at the house. "I'll let you get back inside. I'll keep after Gibson and you keep me in the loop on what you find."

Cole nodded and instead of facing Alyssa and the twins, he looked out over the ocean swells angrily pounding against the shore. A storm was brewing. Usually that comforted him, but tonight it only added to his turmoil.

He didn't want storms anymore. He wanted the bright hopeful mornings that Alyssa saw unfold over the horizon on her morning runs. He wanted a family like the one sitting on the sofa. But did he want a family badly enough to overcome his issues? To relax and let his guard down to make it happen? Could he even do it if he so chose?

He sighed and lost himself in the waves until he was chilled to the bone. By the time he went inside, the family room was empty. Alyssa was likely putting the twins to bed and Dani sat at the kitchen island, her computer open.

"Have you found anything on Gibson's phone?" Cole put his laptop on the table and opened it.

"No luck yet." Dani swiveled on her stool. "Is there a problem?"

"Carter can't locate Gibson. Either he's taken off or Saunders got to him."

"I'll make the search my top priority." She turned back to her computer.

Cole opened his email and found replies from all three police chiefs. The deceased in all three cases had meth in their bloodstreams and were known to law enforcement for dealing drugs, but that's where the similarities to Todd's murder ended. Not much to go on. Still, he could have everyone read the emails to see if he missed something. He sent the files to the printer and it whirred into action.

Alyssa came back into the room. "Did you work everything out with Agent Carter?"

Cole wanted to keep this development from her, but she deserved the truth. "Gibson is missing."

Her face blanched. "Missing as in Nolan did something to him?"

Cole shrugged. "It's too early to tell. Saunders could have gotten to Gibson, or he could have simply taken off to avoid prosecution."

She watched him for a moment as if processing the information, then nodded at the end table holding his printer, still spitting out pages. "Is that the information about the murders?"

He nodded. "I've already read the emails but didn't see anything helpful. Maybe if you look at them you'll see something I missed."

She grabbed the pages and, eyes glued to the paper, she dropped into the chair across from him. He focused on his computer but heard her flip pages and set them on the table.

"Oh, no," she said.

Cole looked up in time to catch her digging her phone out of her pocket.

"What is it?" he asked as Dani joined them.

"Nolan's been doing some traveling for work recently. Since he often helped me with the kids, I included his schedule on my calendar." She tapped the screen of her phone and sat back. She tapped a few more times, then her face filled with terror. She held up the emails. "Nolan was in each of these towns the day of the murders. He killed them. All of them."

TEN

Cole listened to the storm pummeling his window and tried to kick off his covers. The fabric of his pajama pants tangled in the sheets before he freed his legs and sat up. The chilly wood floor nipped at his feet and he glanced at the clock. 2:00 a.m. Only thirty minutes since he'd last checked.

He got up and paced the room, his mind working over their latest lead suggesting Saunders was a serial killer. He'd played down the implications of Saunders's travel schedule for Alyssa, but this was the break he'd been hoping for. True, he didn't hope that Saunders had actually killed three people in addition to Todd, but with three more dead, it upped the odds of being able to bring him in without Gibson's testimony.

He neared the door and a loud crash, followed by glass shattering, sounded from the family room. He grabbed his gun from the nightstand and eased into the hallway. His room was closest to the living areas, and he could see Derrick standing in the family room, his weapon drawn. He suddenly took off, moving out of view.

Was he chasing a suspect?

A door opened behind Cole, and he spun. Dani stepped out of her room, her gun cradled in her hands.

Alyssa poked her head out of the next door. "What is it?"

"Not sure. I'll check it out. Dani, take Alyssa into the kids' room and wait for my all-clear."

Dani nodded and directed Alyssa down the hall. Once the bedroom door was firmly closed, Cole flattened his back against the wall and eased down the hallway, his bare feet making no noticeable sound. He heard rain beating against the front window, but the howling wind sounded loud. Too loud, making him think the window had shattered and rain was pouring in.

At the end of the hallway, he confirmed

the broken window and saw a large rock in a plastic bag on the floor. The front door was flung wide and there was no sign of Derrick. Cole suspected his brother had indeed gone after whoever heaved the rock through the window. Cole wouldn't follow and risk Derrick firing at him. So he waited and looked at the rock. Something white, perhaps paper, lined the bag.

Probably another warning.

He saw movement in the doorway and took a defensive stance.

"We're clear," Derrick announced and flipped on the overhead light.

The glare blinded Cole for a moment before he could make out Derrick lowering the hood of a dripping slicker.

"I'll get some shoes on and tell Dani we're clear," Cole said. "Can you check the garage for something to board up the window?"

Derrick nodded though Cole could tell he wanted to look at the item nestled in the bag with the rock. So did Cole, but he'd slice his feet open on shards of glass if he crossed the room without shoes.

He went down the hall and softly called to

Dani, not wanting to wake the twins if they'd slept through the disaster. She opened the door and came into the hallway. Alyssa stood in the doorway.

Cole hated to give her more bad news, but he couldn't very well hide the shattered window. "Someone threw a rock through the window."

A strangled cry slipped from Alyssa's lips. Dani simply lifted an eyebrow.

"Looks like there's a message with it. You should both get some shoes on to protect yourselves from the broken glass and meet me in the family room." Cole didn't waste time rushing back to his room, where he traded his pajamas for jeans, slipped into his shoes and clipped his holster on his belt to free up his hands.

Back in the family room, he went straight to the rock. Glass shards crunched under his feet and the driving rain dampened his clothing. He grabbed the bag and moved out of the rain. He used the hem of his shirt to open the bag. Better to be careful than to destroy any fingerprints that might've survived the rain. He pulled out a white piece of paper, then carefully set the bag on the table to process later as evidence.

The garage door opened. Cole spun, letting the rock fall and putting his free hand on his weapon.

Derrick entered and wiped his boots on the rug. "Nothing in the garage for boarding the window."

"We have plywood at our office for emergencies at our rental properties," Alyssa said as she joined them, Dani following. They'd both changed into jeans, T-shirts and shoes.

"I have a key so we can go get it," Alyssa added.

Dani met Cole's gaze. "Alyssa shouldn't go out. Derrick and I can go."

Cole studied his sister to see if this was another attempt at matchmaking, but she was focused on the job and alert. He held up the bag with the note. "Before you go, you might want to read this."

Everyone crowded around him, and he unfolded the page by the edges. The white copy paper held colorful letters cut from magazines.

I'm not playing games, Alyssa. Back off on this investigation or you will surely die.

Alyssa's hand shot up to cover her mouth.

"With all the work that went into cutting and pasting these letters we're sure to get a good print or even some DNA." Dani took the paper. "We need to preserve it in something waterproof."

"Why not put it back in the bag it came in?" Alyssa asked.

"The bag will need to be processed for prints and so we need to separate the pieces of evidence." Dani went into the kitchen.

"If you'll get the office key, we'll get going," Derrick said to Alyssa.

They both sounded unfeeling, as if they hadn't noticed Alyssa's shock. Just like Cole had done earlier. Which meant they were both worried and didn't feel able to comfort her. Cole laid a hand on Alyssa's arm and squeezed. She looked up at him, tears filling her eyes, but soon resolve took over. She squared her shoulders and his hand fell away.

"I'll just be a minute," she said and headed back down the hall.

Derrick strode to the door and traded his slicker for a warmer waterproof jacket.

Cole followed him. "We'll clean up this glass while you're gone so it'll be easier to put up the plywood."

"Yeah, you will," Dani joked as she joined them again.

After all the attempts Dani had made to brighten his mood in the past few years, he knew she had the same goal right now. But he couldn't seem to let go of the memory of Alyssa's terrified expression.

"Come on, bro." Derrick clapped Cole on the back. "This is good news. If they're still trying to warn her off they aren't ready to kill her yet."

Alyssa gasped from behind him, and Cole glared at Derrick.

"Nice one." Dani socked Derrick in the arm.

"Let me write down directions to the office and give you the security code." Alyssa handed the keys to Dani and went into the kitchen.

Cole leaned closer to his siblings. "Do a little recon on the way out of the area to make certain our visitor is gone."

They both nodded and Dani slipped into her jacket.

Alyssa returned with the directions and gave them to Dani. "The security code is on the top of the page. The keypad is just inside the door and the plywood is in an office in the back. Any questions?"

After a quick shake of the head, they left and Cole secured the door behind them. "I'll get started on cleaning this up."

Alyssa looked at the window and shuddered.

"Hey." Cole stepped closer and rubbed her arms, though he knew the shiver wasn't from the cold.

"The phone message was one thing, but seeing this one. Here. Where my kids are…" She shuddered again.

Cole knew better, but he couldn't stop himself. He pulled her into his arms and settled her head against his chest. Despite the raging storm and danger lurking all around them, with his arms wrapped around Alyssa he felt more at peace than he'd felt in years.

* * *

Cole's heart beat solidly under Alyssa's ear. She felt protected. Safe. Secure. Exactly the way she'd imagined it would feel to have his arms around her, and she didn't want to move away. But nothing had changed. She still didn't know him and that meant she couldn't fully trust him.

She leaned back, and met his gaze. He watched her for long moments, his eyes prying deep inside. The cold barreling in through the open window fell away, and she felt like she was melting into a puddle. He bent down, his breath soft on her cheek.

"I don't want you to worry," he whispered and it felt like a caress. "We'll resolve this before anyone else gets hurt."

He looked like he was going to kiss her, and she knew she should pull herself free before she did something she'd regret, but she couldn't move. He reached up and tucked a strand of hair behind her ear. His touch was whisper-soft and she shivered. He smiled as if he liked the way she'd responded to him.

"Mom," Riley's sleepy voice came from

behind and Alyssa jerked free. "What happened?"

She hurried over to him before he walked into the room with bare feet. "The window broke in the storm. What're you doing awake?"

"I had to go to the bathroom." He yawned and rubbed his eyes.

"Let's get you back to bed so I can help clean up this mess." She slid the hair off his forehead and led him down the hall.

"Won't the rain keep coming inside?"

"Derrick and Dani are going to board up the window."

"Cool! Can I watch?"

"Sorry, but you need to get some sleep. You have school tomorrow."

"Aw," he said.

She tucked him into his bed. He was asleep again almost as soon as his head hit the pillow. She pulled his covers up and then turned to Brianna to do the same thing. At the doorway, she paused to look at her precious children.

How could she even be thinking about starting something romantic with Cole when she didn't really know him? She wouldn't ever subject her kids to another man who could betray and hurt them.

She returned to the family room and found Cole with a push broom, dustpan and large outdoor garbage can. She approached him and the glass ground under her feet. He looked up from scooping a mound into the dustpan. "Everything okay with the little man?"

"Fine." She took the broom from him and started sweeping. "I guess this is where you say I told you so."

"Told you so?"

"Yeah. You were right about all these windows making the house hard to defend."

"I was right…but wrong, too." He stood and appraised her for a few moments. "Buying a house isn't about defending yourself or even those you love. It's about making a home with them."

Her mouth fell open at his sudden reversal.

He chuckled, his eyes lighting with laughter. "Don't look so shocked. A guy can change his mind, can't he?"

"Yeah, but this is a *big* change."

"Watching you and the twins the past few

days reminded me of my family growing up." He got a faraway look on his face. "Our dad was a cop, but he didn't spend time or energy worrying about keeping us safe from every possible danger. Not that he was reckless. He taught us how to stay safe, then trusted God to take care of all of us and provide our needs."

"Sounds like you want to have a big family yourself."

"I did. Once. But now?" He shrugged and went back to picking up glass, ending the conversation, but she wouldn't let it drop.

"Now?" she asked firmly.

"Now it's time to quit talking about things that might never be and get this mess cleaned up." He turned his back and kept working, clearly ending the discussion.

She didn't know how to feel about his abrupt refusal to answer. Her heart broke for his obvious pain and angst, but after the tender moment they'd shared when they'd hugged, she expected he might actually open up and tell her something about himself.

But why? her mind screamed. Todd and

Nolan both carried deep secrets. What made her think that any man she was attracted to would be any different?

ELEVEN

The morning sun poured through the open window as a small crane lifted a large plate of glass into the gaping hole. Alyssa watched Cole chat with the supervisor of the work crew. He smiled and joked like he had with the twins while he'd helped her get them ready for school. He'd even joked with his siblings and with the Astoria police chief when he'd call to say they could come by to talk to him today.

But that wall Cole erected at the end of their conversation last night stood tall and strong between them, making her upset. Upset with him for being so cool and at herself for hoping he'd be otherwise.

He shook the supervisor's hand then turned and caught her watching him. She met his gaze and waited to see if he intended to shut her out again. He crossed the room, running a hand through his hair and drawing in a deep breath as if he felt a need to fortify himself before talking to her.

"It's good to see the plywood gone," she said, hoping small talk would help them break the ice. "Nothing better than watching the waves in the morning sun."

"We are *so* different." He sat next to her on the sofa. "I like the stormy nights best."

"Maybe if you worked through whatever's eating at you, you could find joy in the morning sun, too."

For a long moment, he simply stared ahead. "I'm sorry about last night. I shouldn't have clammed up on you like that. I've kind of gotten used to keeping things to myself."

She wanted to assure him that she understood, but she still didn't get why he felt a need to hide everything from her.

"C'mon." He grinned at her, but for once his boyish grin didn't make her cave. "At least consider accepting my apology."

She would forgive him, but she wouldn't forget the boundaries he'd set. Maybe she shouldn't keep trying to get him to open up.

Maybe the wall he'd erected between them was a good thing. Especially with the hug last night when she'd heard his heart match the thundering of hers. She couldn't handle falling for the wrong man again.

"Brianna was so cute this morning," he said, his tone far more lighthearted. "Actually both of your kids are really something. You've done an amazing job in raising them."

"If you think you can get in my good graces by complimenting my kids." She paused and looked into his eyes. Contrite, apologetic eyes begging for forgiveness, she couldn't withhold. "I guess you can."

The devastating smile he'd trained on her that first night stole across his face and her heart melted all over again. But she wouldn't let him get to her. She'd keep the conversation on the kids. "You're right. They are amazing. Especially considering all they've been through. I only hope it doesn't scar them permanently."

"Kids are resilient. I remember when Derrick first joined our family. He acted a lot like Riley. All grown up. Thinking of Dani first and protecting her." Cole smiled. She could tell he had fond memories of growing up with his siblings. "He's still protective of her, but after a little while with us, he relaxed. Riley will, too."

"You're going to make a good dad someday," she said.

He frowned. "I only hope I'd be half as good as my adoptive father. Everything I am today is because of him."

"It's great that you had such a strong role model. I wish Todd had been better for the twins. He did his best until he moved out, but then he didn't stop by to see them at all."

Cole's brow rose. "You weren't together when he died?"

"No. We'd taken a break a few weeks before he was killed."

"I know it's none of my business, but if this is related to his murder I'll need to know why he left."

She didn't want to tell him about Todd. It had nothing to do with his murder. But she also didn't want to behave the same way Cole had last night and shut him out. "Todd hit me."

"He what?"

"Hit me. Just once. After a particularly bad day on the job."

He studied her then, long and hard, before he lifted his hand to cup her face. "I don't care if he had the worst day of his life. Hitting you is inexcusable."

Loving the softness of his touch when she shouldn't, she sat back before she did something she'd regret and his hand fell.

"I'm not making excuses for Todd. Just telling you that he let his job get to him and he snapped. He'd wanted to quit his job for a while, but we needed the money." She shook her head. "Twins are expensive, you know? Anyway, we were in debt and he took a second job to help pay the bills. It got to be too much for him to handle."

"Do you think it's possible he took an easy way out and joined Saunders's drug operation?"

"If he did, our finances never reflected that."

"Maybe splitting with you put him over the edge, and he was just getting involved with Saunders when he killed him."

"I guess it's possible, but the other night Nolan said he framed Todd."

"That doesn't mean Todd wasn't involved."

"I just don't think he was." He opened his mouth, but she raised a hand before he said anything. "I know Todd wasn't the man I married and I know Nolan isn't the man I thought he was. So yeah, I'm a horrible judge of men. But for my children's sake, I need to believe their father didn't do anything illegal and we'll be able to clear his name."

Cole covered her hand with his. "I'll do my best to find evidence that clears him."

The supervisor approached them. Cole looked bothered by the interruption, but he stood anyway.

"You shouldn't have any problems with the glass. If you do, give me a call." He held out an invoice.

"Thanks for coming so quickly," Cole said and walked the man to the door.

Alyssa had to repair windows at some of her properties in the past and she'd never gotten this kind of rapid response. But then, Cole was a man who was used to getting things done. Strong, powerful, in charge. Everything she found attractive in a man and everything she needed to keep fighting against if she didn't want to make another mistake.

Cole exited Oregon's scenic Coastal Highway, leaving behind the roaring ocean for Young's Bay on the south side of Astoria. For the thirty-minute drive, he'd focused on the road while Alyssa stared past him at waves crashing on the rocky shoreline. The silence between them was uncomfortable and he wanted to find something to talk with her about, but their discussions weren't often comfortable.

He glanced at her again. He wanted to leave his past behind more than ever to see if this interest between them could develop into something. He'd made a few baby steps in the right direction. Could he take it even further?

Not alone, he couldn't. He needed help. Alyssa's help? God's help? Both probably. But with the police station just ahead, he'd have to table his thoughts for now.

After parking, he checked the mirrors one last time, but there was no real reason to do so. The police station sat on a dead-end street and if a car had taken the exit with him, he would've noticed. He escorted Alyssa inside and gave their information to the front desk clerk.

The chief met them in a few short minutes. An old friend of Cole's dad, he'd aged since Cole had last seen him at his parents' funeral. His gray hair had thinned, his stomach paunch was larger and, though he was as tall as Cole, his stooped shoulders made him appear shorter. He'd been a vibrant go-getter when he'd partnered with Cole's dad on the Portland police force.

Cole shook his hand. "Good to see you again, Chief."

"I was surprised when you called." Chief gripped his hand and patted him on the shoulder with the other. "But I'm glad you did." He released Cole. "Come on back to my office and we can talk in private."

Cole and Alyssa followed him down a dark hallway to an office that held many souvenirs of his years on the Portland and then the Astoria force.

"I don't know how much help I can be, but I'm glad to answer your questions." Chief sat, locked his hands together and settled them over his belly.

"In your email, you said Arturo Cruz's body was found in a landfill," Cole said. "Can you elaborate on that?"

Chief nodded. "It was the oddest thing, really. A worker was supervising the unloading of a truck. A suitcase tumbled out and rolled down the trash heap, landing on his foot. It was heavy and he hoped he'd find something valuable inside. Instead, he found the body and called us."

Cole saw Alyssa blanch and he wished he could've had this conversation without her. "Can you tell me more about the victim?"

"He was a small Hispanic guy. Bruising on his neck says he was strangled from behind. Medical examiner says the bruising indicates the killer was taller than the vic. Plus he thinks the chokehold is a common defensive move taught to military or law enforcement personnel."

Saunders. Cole shared a knowing look with Alyssa. "How tall was the deceased?"

"Five-seven."

Saunders was close to Cole's height so this

fit. "Did you recover any forensic evidence other than the suitcase?"

Chief scoffed. "You try deciding what's important and what you should collect at a dump."

He had a point. Not an easy crime scene to process. "Did you call in help from the state police or sheriff's department?"

Chief raised a brow. "Didn't see how they'd be able to do anything more than I did."

Cole couldn't believe what he was hearing. The officer Cole once knew would be the first to bring in whatever resources he'd need for an investigation. This man sitting across from him more resembled a small-town cop set on protecting his territory.

With Alyssa's life on the line, Cole couldn't ignore the attitude. "Trained forensic specialists are always a good idea on a homicide."

Chief sat forward, his boots hitting the floor with a thump. "I may have been friends with your father, Cole, but I won't have you questioning my judgment like that."

Cole had every reason to question his judgment, but he needed Chief's cooperation if he was going to investigate this case. "I meant no disrespect, Chief. I let my frustrations with this case get the best of me and I apologize." Cole paused and smiled at him. "Have you been able to pin down where the garbage truck picked up the suitcase?"

Chief pulled out a map from his desk and drew a circle with a red pen before sliding it over to Cole. "Best we can tell, the pickup occurred in this two-mile radius. It's a commercial part of the route so we're surmising the suitcase was dropped in one of the many Dumpsters in the area."

"Great," Cole said. "Okay if I take this map?"

"Knock yourself out."

"Would you be willing to let us look at the suitcase before we go?"

"Don't suppose that'd be a problem." He pushed to his feet.

Cole gestured for Alyssa to precede him and they followed Chief down the hallway to a door labeled Evidence. Chief unlocked the door, jerked a suitcase off a lower shelf and dumped it on a long table.

"There you go," he said, dragging the zipper open.

"You wouldn't have a pair of gloves I could wear would you?" Cole asked casually, though he was fuming inside.

Chief had gotten sloppy. Letting two civilians near the evidence like this didn't speak well to his investigative tactics. And letting them touch it—not to mention touching it himself—without gloves? That was just plain negligent.

Who else might he have let do the same thing? If Nolan had killed this guy, they'd need the suitcase to make the case and a defense attorney could have a field day with the sloppy investigation tactics.

Chief dug out a box of latex gloves from under a counter and let them fall on the table with a thud. His phone rang and he pulled it from his belt clip. "Excuse me a minute." He moved to the far side of the room and turned his back to them as he held a low conversation.

Cole ignored him and focused on the suitcase. He snapped on gloves then searched every inch of the interior. Even after weeks of sitting in the open, the bag still reeked of death and rotting garbage. Though soiled, the inside of the bag was unworn. He pulled out paper stuffing from the pockets and showed it to Alyssa.

"Suitcase looks almost new, doesn't it?" he said, keeping his voice as low as Chief's.

"I thought the same thing when I saw that plastic thingy." She pointed at the handle. "Looks like it was left from a price tag."

"And you think that's significant?"

She shrugged. "Maybe the owner was just sloppy, but if I got a new suitcase I'd cut off the tag before using it."

"Good point. Maybe the killer bought the suitcase for the sole purpose of disposing of the body." He tried to keep the excitement out of his voice, but there it was.

"And that's significant why?"

"If we can figure out where this brand of suitcase is sold, maybe the store has security footage of the killer making the purchase."

Alyssa moved closer. "So how do we do find out which stores sell it?"

Cole looked closer and found a zipper housing the roller mechanism. He unzipped it and found a white UPC tag inside. "You have anything to write with in your purse?"

She nodded.

"Write this down." Cole lifted the tag so she could see it but didn't say anything to let Chief know what he was up to. Cole was all for helping Chief solve his case, but if Saunders was the killer, Cole didn't want Chief, who'd proved he'd gotten sloppy, inadvertently alerting Saunders so he could flee.

As Chief said goodbye, Cole noted the manufacturer of the suitcase then turned.

"Thanks for your help." Cole stripped off the gloves and shook hands again with Chief. "I'll let you know if we find anything to help with your case."

"You do that, son," Chief said, his face filled with amusement as if he couldn't imagine Cole could help him.

Cole said his goodbyes and let his excitement over a lead propel him out of the building. As he opened the car door for Alyssa and she got settled, he dug his phone from his pocket and dialed his office.

"The Justice Agency," his sister Kat answered with enthusiasm.

"Hey, Kit Kat. Got something I need you to track down." He rattled off the suitcase details. "Think you can find out where it's sold?"

"Do birds sing?" she replied cheerfully.

Cole smiled at her attitude. Ever since she'd been engaged to Mitch Elliot she'd been like a singing bird herself. "No matter what Ethan has you working on, this is top priority."

"I'll tell him you said that."

"If he has a problem with it, make sure you tell him I said it's too bad." He laughed again and she chuckled along with him.

"You making any progress on this case? Other than falling for this Alyssa woman?"

"Where'd you get an idea like that?" he said, but as he headed to his side of car, the answer came to him. "No need to explain. Dani's been spreading gossip again."

"She doesn't gossip. Just shares her opinion." Kat paused for a long moment. "Which I might add, is usually right on target."

As Cole climbed into the car, he glanced at Alyssa. He knew if he denied his interest in her, he'd be lying so he said his goodbyes.

Back on the highway, Alyssa turned her attention to the window again, and he was thankful for the quiet to think about Kat's comment. It was time to admit he had a thing for Alyssa. It was also time to admit he'd been lonely lately. He'd avoided all that mattered in life. Friends, family, a woman to share his day with. If he ever wanted to let go of the loneliness he had to change. The question was, how did he begin?

Cole had been flexing the muscle in his jaw for the last thirty minutes of their drive and Alyssa wondered if he was mulling over something about the case. Maybe something Kat had said on the phone. Could it be about Frank Gibson? They hadn't discussed him since last night when Cole told her he'd gone missing.

"Have you heard anything about Frank today?" she asked.

"Not yet." He pulled to a stop at the red light near his rental house. "But I'm hoping he's simply lying low and he'll get in touch with Agent Carter soon."

"And if he doesn't?"

"Then I'll send Derrick to find him," he answered.

She loved hearing the confidence in his

voice. She believed nothing could best this man and he could solve any problem he faced.

She gave him an earnest smile. "As usual, it sounds like you have everything under control."

"You really are a positive person, aren't you?" The light changed and he eased the SUV into motion. "I mean, you've faced a lot of hurdles in your life and you still look on the bright side."

"I try."

"No, you do more than try." He glanced at her. "You do it. I wish I could be half as successful at it as you are. What's your secret?"

"No secret really. Just something I learned to do after Todd died."

"Care to share it?"

"It's simple really. One day when everything seemed to go wrong and I was at the end of my rope, I decided I had a choice. I could focus on what was wrong in my life and be miserable. Or I could focus on God and let Him solve my problems and be happy."

"And are you? Happy, that is?"

She laughed. "Yeah, I guess I am. I'm not successful at it all the time. I fall back into my old ways often. Especially when something first hits me. But the thing is, when you focus on the problem, it keeps getting bigger and bigger in your mind. Then it seems overwhelming."

He seemed to be absorbing what she was saying.

"Don't misunderstand me," she added. "The problem doesn't disappear. You still have to deal with it and the effects on your life. And I don't stop worrying completely once I commit a problem to God. But when I catch myself heading in the wrong direction, I recommit the problem and start over again."

"How did you get so wise at your young age?"

"I'm not the wise one. A counselor I saw after Todd died shared a verse he uses in his own life. It's Isaiah 26:3, which basically says we can have perfect peace if we trust in God and keep our minds on Him."

He turned into the driveway of the house. "I wish I could do that," he said and shifted into Park. "You have no idea how much I wish I could," he added in almost a whisper.

The torment in his voice made her heart

constrict. Despite warning bells saying touching him would be a huge mistake, she rested her hand on his arm. "We could pray about it. Together."

He looked at her like she'd lost her mind. "I'm not much into prayer these days." He patted her hand then opened his door and climbed out.

Sadness seeped into her heart. He was as troubled as Todd had been—maybe even more troubled. She bent her head and offered a prayer for him to find peace in the midst of his turmoil.

He opened her car door. "I'm hoping Kat will locate the purchase info for the suitcase, but we can't pin all of our hopes on one lead. So I'm going to continue researching the other murders."

"I can help with that," she offered on their walk to house. "That is, if I can find where Riley left my computer this morning."

"I saw him put it on the kitchen counter." Cole unlocked the door and stood back.

She stepped inside the warm, inviting space that was starting to feel familiar and comfortable to her. As was Cole and his family. She thought about how he helped her ready the kids for school this morning. She loved having someone to help her wrangle the twins. To share her difficulties. What a support network this wonderful family would be.

She headed for the kitchen but stopped dead in her tracks and felt the blood draining from her face.

He'd been here. In the house while they were gone.

"Nolan was here." She pointed with a trembling finger at the large bullet sitting upright on the countertop. "He did this."

Cole took one look at the counter and jerked out his gun. "Stay here and don't move. I need to make sure he's not still in the house."

Alyssa nodded but couldn't take her eyes off the shiny copper-and-gold bullet standing on the granite. She didn't know anything about bullets, but this one was several inches long so she guessed it came from a rifle or shotgun. Someone, probably Nolan, had neatly printed her first name in black marker on the side.

He'd left nothing else on the counter—just the casing—but a shiver started at Alyssa's head and worked down her body. Nolan didn't need to leave a note to get his message across. He had a bullet with her name on it and if she didn't back off he would end her life.

TWELVE

Alyssa walked out of the family room and Cole forced himself to remain seated at the dining room table and not follow her. After he'd cleared the house, he'd grilled Derrick about why he hadn't heard Saunders break into their home. Cole wanted to blame Derrick, but it wasn't his fault. He was simply getting the rest he'd need to do his job tonight.

Cole's phone rang, and he spotted Kat's name on caller ID. "I could really use some good news, Kit Kat."

"Then you'll be glad I called. The suitcase is sold exclusively at SuperMart. And before you ask, I've already checked and there are two SuperMarts in Astoria."

"Hold on while I get the map from Chief." Cole pressed the speaker button and set down his phone then dug through his case folder. He folded the map to display the red ring Chief had circled. "Okay, go ahead, Kat."

She gave him the first address.

He scanned the circle. "I don't see the store in our target area."

"Here's the other address."

He ran his finger over the map. "Bingo. It's on the fringe. Now all I need to do is get SuperMart's security team to talk to me."

"Already done," she said, pride ringing through her words.

"How?"

"Mitch has a cousin in management at SuperMart. He's already talked to her. When you get to the store tell the head of security to call Patti Fisk, and she'll approve whatever you need."

"You're the best, Kit Kat. The very best."

"Don't you know it." He heard her laughing as he disconnected.

Excited about the lead, Cole went in search of Alyssa. He found her in the kids' bedroom making one of the beds. The sight of her engaged in such a simple task warmed his heart.

He was certain she had been and would be a great wife. One Todd Wells hadn't deserved.

He stayed in the doorway watching, enjoying the way she'd found peace after her initial fear from the bullet. She'd done exactly what she'd said in the car. By the time Cole had come back from clearing the house, he'd found her head bowed, offering her problem to God. Cole was so impressed with her transformation that he'd stopped and prayed, too. He wasn't sure he would get an answer, but he felt better after offering up his concerns.

She turned and caught his eyes on her, her cheeks coloring and a shy look stealing over her face. "How long have you been standing there?"

"Not long." He shouldn't keep watching her, but she radiated a vitality that drew him like a magnet and he was powerless to look away.

The blush consumed her face and she blew out a breath, her hair lifting with the force of air. "So did you have something you wanted or do you just like watching me make beds?"

"Both," he answered without thinking.

A quick flash of interest lit her eyes before she veiled it. "What did you want?"

He took a breath himself and waited for the charged atmosphere to calm. "We have a lead." He told her about SuperMart. "I'd like to head up there now to see the security tapes."

"It's nice to have good news for once." Her phone rang and her concentration shifted to the phone. She stared at the screen, a frown forming. "Sorry. I have to take this. It's my office."

"I'll wait for you in the other room." He went to the family room to give her privacy. Pacing the length of the room, he wondered how to deal with the obvious attraction between them. Ignoring it wasn't helping— and it didn't make the feelings go away. And now...now what? Did he have the courage to move forward? To bury the past and consider a relationship?

He heard her footsteps coming down the hall and he warned himself not to get carried away. For now, he'd stay cautious and see how things went.

"That was the alarm company for one of

my rental properties," she said coming into the room. "The fire sensor issued a trouble warning. With renters arriving tomorrow, I need to reset the panel. Would it be okay if we stop on the way to Astoria? It'll only take a few minutes."

He opened his mouth to tell her he didn't think it was a good idea, but she rushed on. "I really hate to ask but the rental income will keep the owner out of foreclosure."

"Can't someone else in your office do this?"

"Yeah, but if Sam loses out on this rent and the bank takes over, I want to be able to look him in the eye and tell him I did everything I could to prevent it from happening."

Of course she would. That was the kind of woman he was coming to know her to be. She was caring. Thoughtful. And irresistible when she spoke passionately, as she was doing now. Her eyes were wide and alert. Her face animated. Her posture determined.

"Please?" she asked and laid a hand on his sleeve.

He felt her touch all the way to his heart and it took everything he was made of not to sweep her into his arms like he had last night.

Don't lose focus on the job, he told himself.
Run through a threat assessment.

Could he let her do this? Would she be safe?
A trouble alarm was usually a simple glitch in
the system and a quick reset fixed the problem. He supposed Saunders could have tampered with the sensor, but he wasn't likely to
attack in broad daylight. Plus, he'd just left
his little warning and Alyssa had done nothing to make him think she wasn't backing
off. So Cole doubted Saunders had anything
to do with this issue.

"It should be okay," Cole said and hoped
he wasn't making a mistake.

"Thank you, Cole." She jumped up and
threw her arms around his neck.

At first he didn't respond, but she tightened
the hug and he slid his arms around her waist,
drawing her close. He would've pulled back
and looked into her amazing eyes, but she
suddenly let go and stood back.

Her face was flushed and her breathing
rapid. "Sorry about that. I got carried away.
I'll call my office to confirm and change into
something more professional for our meeting.
Then we can go."

Cole sat behind his computer and checked his emails until Alyssa came back into the room. She'd traded dark-wash jeans and a bright red top for black dress slacks and a tailored blue blouse. She'd pulled her hair into a bun and looked regal and cool. But there was nothing cool about this woman. She was warm, caring, compassionate. And beyond gorgeous. He was attracted to her beauty. What man wouldn't be? But it was her heart and positive attitude that made him forget everything happening around him. Forget his problems and believe in hope. Believe he might have everything he wanted in life.

"Ready." She smiled at him, drawing him out of his musings.

He gave a clipped nod and stepped outside, letting the cool afternoon breeze wash over him. He made sure the area was clear then escorted her to the car. She plugged the rental property's address in the GPS and he concentrated on driving, following directions to a small home in a well-kept neighborhood.

"Stay here while I make a quick security sweep." He hopped out and alternated his search of the property with keeping an eye on her. When he had to move out of her sight he hurried but didn't cut corners in confirming the house was secure.

Back at the car, he opened her door. "Straight up to the house and inside, okay?"

She nodded. Though there were no cars or people moving in the neighborhood, he kept his head on a swivel while they strolled up the walkway. A rare sun break beamed down on them, yet the chilly wind whipping off the ocean reinforced his apprehension about this trip.

He faced the road while she worked the lockbox. The snap as it popped free ricocheted though the quiet neighborhood. He heard the firm click of the key settling into the lock and the squeaky door groaned open. An odd clicking noise followed.

He spun around and took in a deep breath. Gas? The IED exploding and Mac catapulting through the air flashed into Cole's brain. He grabbed Alyssa's arm. "Run."

"What?" she asked as he literally dragged her down the walkway.

"Gas explodes," he said and sped up, tugging her at a speed she struggled to match.

"It's okay. Sam's absentminded. He probably forgot to turn off the gas on the fireplace."

His mind screamed that it wasn't Sam and if they didn't get moving faster, they could die. He scooped her into his arms.

"But—" she said and he ignored her need to talk, pounding across the street toward the ditch.

"I'm sure this is just—" Her words disappeared in an ear-shattering explosion.

A flash of light brighter than any of the explosions he'd witnessed in the past spiraled into the air while a concussive wave pummeled his back. He dove into the ditch, landing on his side to keep from crushing Alyssa. Burning metal pierced his back. Pain screamed along his nerve endings, but he ignored it and completely covered her body. A sharp object sliced through his forehead and he lowered his head. He could feel the swift beat of Alyssa's heart and hear her quick breaths mixed with the sounds of debris landing all around.

He flashed back to Iraq. To Mac. To that day. That horrible, horrible day. Digging out of the rubble. Scrambling back in to find Mac. His body lifeless, his eyes staring blankly ahead.

"Cole," Alyssa said, the terror in her voice bringing him back.

"It's okay," he whispered and wondered if it really was.

Items kept hitting his back as regret over his decision to bring Alyssa here swamped him. The explosion wasn't a case of Sam leaving the gas on. More likely, Nolan had tried to kill Alyssa. Gas needed a spark to ignite, and the click he'd heard when the door opened was likely for a timer. The timer would give them enough time to get into the house and then it would create a spark to trigger the explosion. They'd been lucky—the timer had also given them a few seconds to run for cover.

So odd, when Saunders's warning was only a few hours old, but criminals acted unpredictably.

"Cole, can we get up now?" Alyssa's voice broke into his thoughts, and he lifted his head to look around.

All that remained of the right half of the house were timbers, burning with bright flames. The left side stood intact, although fire spread rapidly toward it. His car was pinned under the garage door, but it hadn't caught fire.

He pushed to a crouching position. Eyes wide with panic, Alyssa stared at him. She took deep breaths, but fear seemed to be winning out.

He took her hand. It was cold and clammy. "We took quite a tumble. Are you okay?"

"You blocked the fall. I'm fine, but you're bleeding." She reached for his forehead, her hand trembling, but then let her hand drop.

"It's nothing." He waved her off.

"It doesn't look like nothing." She took a shuddering breath and looked around as if she expected another attack.

He'd like to hold her until her fear subsided, but he had to arrange for backup in case Saunders planned to finish the job.

"Take a minute to catch your breath. I'm going to call this in." After squeezing her hand, he stood and took a few steps away so she couldn't hear his conversation with Derrick. Neighbors had stepped onto the street and he knew they would phone 911.

"We have an incident," he said after Derrick answered. He told his brother about the explosion and gave him the address. "I need you to get over here. My car isn't drivable and I don't want Alyssa out in the open any longer than it takes to give her statement to the police. Plus, I definitely don't trust the responding officers to take her home."

"I'm on my way."

"Come prepared," Cole added. "Prepared" in their world meant ready to defend themselves with force if necessary. "Alert Dani to the increased threat and have her phone Carter at the DEA. I want an impartial investigator out here before Saunders tampers with any evidence that could incriminate him."

Derrick agreed and Cole hung up. He picked his way through debris to Alyssa, who'd come to a sitting position. She still seemed dazed, and he hated to make it worse, but he had to warn her that Nolan would likely respond to the fire.

He squatted next to her. "You doing okay?"

"As much as I can be when I was almost blown up." She dug into her pocket and her hand came out with a wad of tissues. "You, however, are bleeding." She pressed the tissues on his forehead.

He winced at the pain, but having something to keep her mind off the blast would help with the shock so he let her continue. "Derrick's on his way and as soon as the police take your statement we'll get out of here. They should arrive any time."

Her hand fell away. "What if Nolan responds?"

"There's a good possibility that he will, so we need to be prepared with the same story."

"Story? What story? We got here and the house blew up. What else can we say?"

"He's going to ask if we have any idea how the house exploded. It's best to stay with the story that you think Sam left the gas on."

"But you don't think that's likely."

"No," he answered, but he didn't go into his theory in case nerves made her slip up and tell Saunders. "When he questions you, he'll be watching to see how you respond to him. Though we know he's on to us, it's still best to act like everything but the explosion is normal."

"I don't think I can do this, Cole." She ran a hand over her face.

"Yes, you can. You're one of the bravest women I know."

"No, I'm not."

He crooked a finger under her chin and lifted her head. "You have withstood things strong women falter under, yet you set an example for everyone in how to keep your faith and stay positive. This is just another one of those things you have to get through. You can do it."

He saw the first police vehicle arrive and hoped Saunders wouldn't follow standard police procedure and separate them until he could take their statements.

Alyssa must have been thinking the same thing. "You won't leave me alone with him?"

"Never," he responded and hoped he'd be able to keep his word.

Alyssa squared her shoulders and walked up to Nolan. He put his hands on her arms and it took iron willpower not to cringe as she lifted her chin to look him in the eye.

"Are you hurt?" he asked. If she didn't

know better, she'd believe he was actually concerned.

"I'm fine. Just shaken up." She offered a shaky smile.

He slid his hands down her arms and drew her into a hug. She forced muscles that wanted to stiffen to relax by pretending they were Cole's arms wrapped around her.

"After what Alyssa's been through, it would be good if I could take her home," Cole said. His comment gave her the excuse she needed to back away. "If you could take our statements right away, that would be helpful."

Nolan appraised him with a raised eyebrow. Cole simply stared back without an ounce of emotion on his face, but Alyssa could see the iron will in his expression.

Nolan turned his focus on her. "Go ahead and tell me what happened."

"It's simple, really. I came to check a fire sensor that was emitting a trouble warning. When we opened the door we smelled gas."

"We decided not to go in the house. We headed across the street for safety and to call it in," Cole added, and she had to admit his simple telling of the facts made the explosion seem far less terrifying.

And if Cole could be so calm and recite the events without any emotions, so could she. "I think Sam must have left the gas on for the fireplace. You know how absentminded he is."

Nolan took a step closer. "Or he didn't want the bank taking his house so he decided to destroy it."

"Sam wouldn't do that."

"Everyone in town knows he was desperate, Alyssa. Desperate men do desperate things."

You ought to know, she thought but kept it to herself.

"Not Sam. He wouldn't do that." She had to remain calm, but she hated that he was disparaging a good man to cover his murderous ways.

"Speculating on the cause of the explosion without any facts won't do any good." Cole put a hand on Alyssa's shoulder. "Now if you don't have any further questions, I'm taking Alyssa home."

"Looks like your car is toast. I'll give her a ride."

"No need. I'm sure you have to process the scene and my brother is waiting right over there." Cole pointed at Derrick, who leaned on the side of his SUV, his arms and feet crossed as if disinterested. But he was a Justice, and Alyssa knew his eyes behind the sunglasses would be darkly intense.

Nolan raised that brow again. "So is your whole family in town looking at houses?"

Cole lifted a shoulder. "Not all of them, but I have the feeling the rest will be here before nightfall."

The threat in his tone was clear, and Alyssa was surprised after his warnings not to give away their suspicions that Cole would taunt Nolan this way.

A loud groan cut through the air, and the house shuddered. The roof collapsed and hit the ground, sending up a cloud of dust. Cole spun, turning his back to Alyssa. A shard of metal protruded through his shirt, dried blood circling the wound.

"Cole. Your back. We need the paramedics to look at it."

"I'm fine. It's just a scratch. We should go." He held out his hand, motioning for her to go first.

His tone said he was more concerned for her safety than his injury. In this mood, she wouldn't get him to cooperate so she held her tongue and hoped when they reached the car she could enlist his brother's help.

At the car, she stopped in front of Derrick. "Cole has a piece of metal the size of a flag pole sticking out of his back and he's refusing medical attention."

"Alyssa," Cole warned. "You're exaggerating."

"Let me see," Derrick said, and though he was the younger brother, Alyssa could see Cole thought twice before ignoring him and opening the door for her.

She crossed her arms. "If you won't listen to reason, then think about my kids. We can't go to SuperMart looking this way, so we'll have to change clothes. They'll be home from school soon and that thing sticking out of your back will scare them to death."

"Fine," Cole grumbled. "As long as you agree to stay in the car while we wait for

Carter to get here, I'll make a stop at the E.R."

"You're not stalling so you won't have to see a doctor, are you?" she asked, her eyebrows raised in suspicion.

He shook his head. "I don't want to leave Saunders unsupervised. He could tamper with evidence."

"Okay, but we're out of here the minute Carter arrives." She climbed in the backseat. Cole and Derrick got in the front. When she saw Cole had to sit sideways in his seat to keep from pressing on the metal, she felt vindicated in insisting on the E.R.

The three of them sat silently. Tension consumed the small space, making it feel like an eternity before Agent Carter arrived, though he drove up within five minutes.

As Carter walked past their car, Cole nodded his acknowledgment then faced his brother. "My mobility is limited. Keep your eyes out for a tail."

"I hate to butt into your business, bro." Derrick pulled onto the street. "But you aren't invincible, you know. Sometimes you have to let people help you."

Derrick's pointed tone said he meant far more than Cole's injury. Alyssa expected Cole to glare at his brother, but he simply gave a defeated nod. Maybe this meant he'd realized he couldn't control everything around him. And maybe it also meant he was ready to talk about that incident in Iraq. When the opportunity to chat with him next presented itself, she'd encourage Cole to open up and make sure he knew she was there to listen.

THIRTEEN

Standing in the security office at SuperMart, Cole pointed at one of the six computer monitors and winced when the movement strained stitches he'd received in the E.R. "Rewind the video. That's Saunders."

"Are you sure?" Alyssa looked up at him from her chair beside the technician named Pete.

"Yes," Cole answered. "I'm positive."

Her face blanched, and Cole knew she was about to lose whatever hope she had left that Saunders wasn't a murderer. She shouldn't be here. Shouldn't have to go through this. Cole wished he'd been able to convince her to stay at the house with his family, but her tenacity in bringing Saunders to justice had her insisting on coming.

The young technician rewound the video for

cash register fifteen. The computer whirred and a fan hummed. Two suitcases matching the make and model they sought had been purchased the night of Arturo Cruz's murder. The computer point of sale system recorded one sale paid by credit card at register twelve and one paid with cash at this register. As a cop, Saunders would know not to leave a trail with a credit card, so Cole had started with the cash transaction.

"Here you go," Pete said.

Cole leaned forward to get a better look. Saunders approached the checkout counter, placed the suitcase on the belt, then moved toward the register. The camera caught a flash of his face before he turned to give the cashier a flirtatious smile.

Alyssa scooted back. "It *is* Nolan."

"Want me to make a copy of the video?" Pete glanced back at Cole.

Cole nodded. "And cue up the second camera for the register to get a better shot of his face."

"I can also bring up the cameras for the exit and parking lot. Might show you the vehicle he's driving."

"Good," Cole said, though the car Saunders drove didn't matter in this case. They had a positive ID and wouldn't need to run DMV records.

As Pete found the right video feed, Cole turned his focus to Alyssa. Her eyes were glued to the screen, and she kept twisting the hem of her shirt between her fingers. He couldn't imagine what she was going through. A man she'd cared for and trusted—had allowed near her children—had killed another person. Maybe more than one. That would shake anyone. Even someone as strong as he knew her to be.

Pete tapped a finger on the top monitor. "This is the second camera on this register."

Saunders stood confident and strong, not a hint of unease over either having just killed a fellow human being or planning to do so in the next few minutes. It took a coldhearted man to stay calm and even flirt with the cashier in that situation.

"I'll take a copy of that, too," Cole told Pete.

"Okay, here's the exit footage." Pete pointed at another monitor.

Saunders calmly strolled toward the store's

exit, pulling the large green suitcase behind him. Cole couldn't be sure, but it looked like Saunders's lips were puckered and he was whistling.

Alyssa shook her head. "He's acting so cocky, like he'll never get caught. He's not even trying to hide his face from the camera."

"Sometimes dirty cops think they're too smart to get caught." Cole didn't take his eyes off the video.

"Here's the parking-lot camera," Pete announced as the top monitor flashed with video of Saunders putting the suitcase in the back of his car.

"Unbelievable." Alyssa's head swung from side to side. "He's driving his official Pacific Bay Police vehicle."

"He's a cop?" Pete exclaimed.

Cole stared down at Pete. "It's crucial to our investigation that you keep quiet about this. Can I trust you to be one of us, Pete, and not tell anyone?"

Pete nodded vigorously.

"Good, I knew I could count on your discretion," Cole said.

Pete puffed out his chest, and his eyes filled with pride. "Anything else you need?"

Cole nodded. "We should take a look at the video from register twelve to cover all of our bases."

Pete went back to work and Alyssa swiveled to face Cole. "You're not thinking this is some kind of coincidence and the other person is who we want, are you?"

"No, but if we want to have Saunders arrested, we have to be thorough."

"Here you go." Pete clicked his mouse. "The first camera's footage."

"It's a woman," Alyssa said.

"And she's way too petite to have committed this crime," Cole answered vaguely, not wanting to share with Pete that their victim had been strangled. "Go ahead and burn those files to a disc for us, Pete, and we'll get out of your way. Thanks."

"Hey." Pete laughed. "Don't rush off on my account. This is the most fun I've had all year."

Cole looked at Alyssa. Pete might be having fun, but she was miserable. The now familiar urge to sweep her into his arms made him take a step closer, but he shoved his hands into his pockets to keep from following through.

Someone had tried to end her life today because he had failed to protect her. Just like Mac. Cole may have let down his wall and let Alyssa give him hope for a wonderful future, but the wall was going back up.

Right here. Right now.

The explosion was a perfect reminder. If he allowed himself to care about someone, he exposed himself to the chance of failing them. And the last thing Alyssa needed was to be led on by another man she couldn't trust.

Staring out the window of his rental home, Cole disconnected his phone call from Agent Carter. Cole had been right. The blast that had destroyed Sam's house was the work of an arsonist who'd set a trigger switch. The arsonist had done a good job of hiding it, and if Carter hadn't brought in an arson investigator, Saunders would've covered up the explosion, blamed it on Sam or made it seem like an accident.

It was also proof positive that Cole's judgment had been off and he'd put Alyssa in harm's way.

"You look tense," Alyssa said from behind.

He couldn't turn and look at her or he would spill his guts, and that wouldn't be good for either of them. "Agent Carter called. He confirmed the arson."

She came to stand next to him. "So either Sam purposefully blew up his house, or Nolan tried to have me killed."

"The trigger device was professionally constructed. Unless Sam has contacts with an experienced arsonist, it was Saunders."

"Sam's the local grocery store owner. I doubt he knows people who start fires."

"Yeah, my thoughts, too."

She finally looked up at him. "And that's why you're so pensive."

He kept his focus out the window. "I should've been more cautious and shouldn't have let you go to the house."

She touched his arm, but he avoided her gaze.

"You can't blame yourself for this, Cole. I

would have gone no matter your decision. I owe my best to Sam."

"Even if it means risking your life?"

"No, of course not. But I thought since Nolan had just warned me, he wouldn't actually try to kill me. Now I know better and won't make that same mistake."

Her attitude was exactly what he feared. Each and every day someone he cared for could make a decision solely based on what they could see and that decision could cost them their lives.

"This is about more than the explosion." She stepped in front of him. As much as he didn't want to look into her eyes, he couldn't look away. "You can tell me if I'm sticking my nose in where it doesn't belong, but this is about Iraq, isn't it?"

He nodded.

"Do you want to talk about it?"

"Want to? Not really. Just like I don't want to think about it, either, but it's there every day."

"What happened?" She put her hand on his arm again, and his first instinct was to move nearer. To trust the intimacy she was offering and share the pain, but he couldn't share his problems and let her in. Not without hurting her.

She inched even closer. "You don't have to tell me, but I'd like to help if I can."

She was trying so hard to help and he was being a jerk for shutting her out like this. He could at least give her a quick accounting. Leave out how he felt and recite the events of the day, as he had with his commanding officers.

He peered through the window at the churning ocean. "We were in the city. Clearing a property thought to house rebels. We split up. Circled the place and worked our way inside." His stomach churned like the waves, but he went on. "I spotted a boy. About Riley's age. His foot was stuck under rubble. I was supposed to keep my eye on the mission. Clear the property, not rescue the boy. But if I left him, there was no telling when someone would find him. He could die."

"So you freed him."

"Yes, and in the time it took me to get his leg free, my buddy Mac finished clearing his section. When I didn't show up at our arranged location, he came looking for me." Cole looked at the large beams in the ceiling and fought back his emotions. "He triggered an IED and lost his life right in front of me. If I'd done my job and stayed focused on the mission, I would've died. Not Mac."

"And now you live your life trying to prevent something like that from happening again," she finished for him. "You can't be responsible for everything, Cole. That's a heavy burden that only God can carry."

"I know that up here." He stabbed his forehead.

"But not in your heart." She laid her hand on his chest and the warmth thawed his resolve to stay away from her. "Stop focusing on the problem, Cole. Let it go and let yourself hope for a better tomorrow."

He gazed into the concern and empathy in her eyes and it was nearly his undoing. She was such an incredible woman. Kind, compassionate, strong, beautiful. Everything he would want in a woman to share his life with.

Without thinking of the consequences, he cupped the side of her face. "You make me want to hope. For the first time in years, I want a life free from guilt and worry."

"Then reach out and take it."

She meant it. Every word. Thought he could do it. And maybe he could with a woman like her by his side. He circled a thumb over her cheek, and their eyes met and held. He shouldn't kiss her, but he needed to as much as he needed to breathe.

He ignored the warning telling him he would only hurt her and lowered his head. Claimed her lips. They were soft and pliable and not at all resistant. She felt this, too. Wanted it, too. But was it good for either of them?

No. Of course not. You'll only hurt her.

He drew back and circled his arms around her, nestling her head against his chest.

They stood there as one until he heard a car pull up, doors slam and her kids laughing as they approached the house. He couldn't let Riley and Brianna find the two of them embracing like this. They'd already had such heartache in their lives and didn't need to wonder if their mother was getting involved with him.

He reluctantly stepped back. After one last glance into Alyssa's compelling eyes, he lifted his head and prayed that once her gentle touch was gone his heart wouldn't close over again.

FOURTEEN

With the twins and Dani at school and Derrick sleeping the next morning, the house was quiet. Too quiet, making Alyssa's mind drift. Sitting across the table from Cole, she couldn't keep her thoughts from that amazing kiss yesterday. All she'd been able to think about for the past thirty minutes was his tender look when he'd lowered his head to kiss her. He was such an incredible man. But scarred and badly hurt inside. She wanted to help him work through it, but she was still wary of committing her heart. Could they really have a future together?

Argh! She jumped up and went to the kitchen to get a cup of coffee. But then what? Go sit next to him again under the guise of researching other murders even though she couldn't focus? That was just asking for trouble. She searched the cheerful room for something to do to keep busy. Dani had done the dishes and cleaned up after breakfast before she took the twins to school.

Maybe Alyssa could bake something. In the burgeoning pantry, she grabbed a chocolate-chip bag, scanned the recipe ingredients and found they had everything she needed to make cookies. She flipped on the oven and set the ingredients on the counter.

Growing up, she'd wanted the kind of mom who'd baked, volunteered at her school and let her have sleepovers. Instead, her mom worked full time and wasn't home until late each night. Alyssa didn't want the same life for her children, but she had to work to support her family.

She sighed and took her frustrations out by mixing all of the ingredients in a large bowl until the dough was smooth and creamy. She finished baking the entire batch in another thirty minutes and a tantalizing aroma filled the house.

Cole came into the kitchen with a little-boy look on his face. "The smell is driving me crazy. Can I have one?"

Despite the earlier tension, she laughed at his hangdog expression and nodded. "Help yourself, but save some for the twins."

He took a bite and groaned. "Our mom used to bake all the time. Kat uses her recipes sometimes but not often enough for my liking."

"Sounds like you really miss your parents."

"They were amazing people." His voice broke, and he polished off the cookie to cover for it. "You've never mentioned your family."

"Nothing to tell, really." She started gathering the baking utensils together and put them in hot, sudsy water. "I think I mentioned that I'm an only child. My parents died in a car crash when I was in college. I loved them and still miss them, but they both lived for their careers so we weren't really close."

"That's too bad," he said, and she could tell he meant it.

She nodded at the cookies. "You should have another one while the chocolate is gooey and warm."

Their eyes met. He didn't look away—as he'd done all morning. Something seemed to shift in his eyes. As if he'd come to a decision of some sort. She wanted to look away, but she couldn't help but wonder what had changed in his mind.

He took a step forward and ran a thumb over her cheek. "Flour."

She loved his touch. Loved having him look at her this way. But she couldn't let her guard down. She stepped back. "I don't think this is a good idea, Cole."

"This, meaning?"

"Whatever this thing is between us isn't a good idea."

"You mean because I'm just here to protect you?"

"I'm not ready for a relationship."

His thumb trailed down her cheek, firing every nerve in her body. His hand settled on her shoulder. "Todd really did a number on you, didn't he?"

"Yes," she said so softly she wasn't sure if he heard her. Truth be told, she didn't want him to or he'd ask questions she wasn't prepared to answer. "But it also seems like you aren't ready for one, either."

"I'm not."

"Iraq?" she asked. "Or did some woman break your heart, too?"

"Both. Together." His hand fell away and he shoved it in his jeans pocket. "I was engaged. We were supposed to get married when my first tour ended. Instead, she sent me a Dear John email the month before my tour ended."

"I'm so sorry, Cole." She sunk her hands into the soapy water in the sink to keep from touching him again. "Long-distance separations can be hard. Did she find someone else?"

"No. She decided she didn't want to be married to a man who worked in law enforcement."

Alyssa could understand that. "Not that I think what she did was right, but maybe it was for the best. Being married to a cop is hard and if she had reservations before the wedding, it would only have gotten worse." She looked up at him. "Trust me, Cole. I know how frightening it can be to see the man you love put his life on the line every day. I'm so sorry she hurt you, though. It must've been hard to break up. Even worse when you were in Iraq."

"That's why I signed up for a second tour."

His hand went around the back of his neck and he massaged. "Which was stupid. I acted impulsively. Ran away from my problems." He shook his head. "I got through the first tour knowing Laura was waiting for mé. The second tour was much worse. Then I lost Mac. Plus we saw far more casualties in that tour. Everyone around us, wounded or dead." He shuddered and looked away. "It's hard to come back from, you know?"

She didn't know—she could only imagine. "I can't begin to understand the horror you saw over there. Or how you felt when your fiancée left you, but I do understand what it's like to lose someone you thought you'd spend the rest of your life with."

"Except you've taken it in stride and moved on. I… Well, I haven't."

Had she moved on?

Not really. Not if she couldn't ever trust a man again. She was stuck in the same dark place as Cole, and she didn't know how to get out of it any more than he did.

Chomping a cookie that now tasted like dust, Cole went back into the family room.

Alyssa didn't want to be married to a man who put his life on the line for others, and Cole would never leave his chosen career. Good. That meant he could finally put aside his feelings for her and focus solely on the case.

"Right," he mumbled. "Good luck with that."

Nearing the window, he caught sight of blue and red lights spiraling into the misty fog near the ocean. He grabbed his binoculars from the closet and zoomed in. Two police cars and an ambulance parked close to the pounding surf, but Cole couldn't make out anything else.

"Do you think someone drowned?" Alyssa asked, coming up beside him.

"It's a little cold to go swimming."

"Some hardy locals swim in wetsuits all year round."

Could be that, but Cole's mind went to far worse possibilities. The twirling sirens were too close to the house for comfort. "I'm going to get Derrick to check it out."

Cole went down the hallway to his brother's room and pounded on the door.

"What?" Derrick grumbled.

Cole went inside. "Sorry to wake you, but we have an incident at the beach that I need you to check out."

He rubbed tired eyes and sat up. "Incident?"

"Ambulance and two patrol vehicles. Could be nothing, but I won't rest until I know."

"Fine. I'll go check." He swung his legs to the floor. "But there better be a cup of coffee waiting for me when I get out there."

"You got it." Cole went straight to the kitchen, but by the time he got there, he could hear the pot dripping.

Alyssa looked up from putting cookies into containers. "I figured after not getting much sleep, Derrick would want some coffee."

She was so considerate. Always thinking of others.

"Listen, Cole," she said. "I hope you didn't misunderstand what I said before."

"Misunderstand what?" He focused on the dripping pot.

"About your former fiancée. What she did to you was horrible, and I don't want you to think I condone the way she broke up with you." She touched his arm in the gentle way she'd taken to doing lately, and he stepped back before he let her overpower his common sense. "I was just trying to say that it's a whole lot easier to realize you aren't meant to be with someone before you get married than after. And it's especially difficult to find out once you have kids."

"I didn't misunderstand." The pot gurgled, and he grabbed a travel cup for Derrick and a mug for himself.

"Oh, okay. Good," she said, but he could tell she was confused by the way he kept waffling in his behavior toward her.

He held out his cup. "You want one?"

"No, thanks."

He went to the pot and poured the rich black liquid, the tantalizing scent snaking into the air and mixing with the cookie aroma. Yawning, Derrick came into the room, and Cole handed him the steaming travel mug.

"Cookies." Derrick smiled at Alyssa and shoved one in his mouth. He washed it down with a sip of coffee and moaned before grabbing another one.

Alyssa smiled back at him, her sweet, soft

smile that Cole loved so much. "Guess that means you like them."

"They're fantastic." He grabbed another and wolfed it down.

"The beach," Cole said pointedly.

"I'm going." Derrick rolled his eyes and grabbed a few more cookies before leaving.

"Thanks for making the coffee." Cole raised his cup. "I'll be at my computer if you need me."

He settled behind the screen but couldn't concentrate on the words, so he sipped his coffee, letting the mug warm his hands while he stared off into space.

His phone rang and he jerked, sloshing coffee on the keyboard. He set down the cup and grabbed his phone. When he saw Derrick's icon, he answered on speaker and put the phone on the table then tipped the laptop over and wiped with a napkin before the moisture settled into the cracks.

"It's not good news, bro," Derrick said.

"What happened?"

"A body washed up on shore."

"And?" Cole asked impatiently, not having any time for his little brother's dramatic pauses.

"It's Officer Gibson."

Alyssa gasped from where she stood on the other side of the room.

"Nolan killed him," she said, crossing the open space.

"Don't jump to conclusions, Alyssa. We don't even know if he was murdered." He looked at his phone. "What are they saying at the scene, Derrick?"

"No obvious sign of foul play. One of the cops said Gibson was an avid swimmer. He swam all year round. They're thinking the rough seas got to him and he drowned."

"And you're thinking it's too coincidental."

"Yeah, aren't you?"

"Yes, but speculation won't get us anywhere, and we won't know anything until an autopsy is performed."

"Which out here in the boonies could take some time."

"So we proceed as if he was murdered." He glanced at his watch. "Dani should be here with the kids any minute, so if you hightail it back here we can have a conversation before they arrive."

"I'm on my way." Derrick disconnected.

Alyssa dropped into a chair. "So with Frank dead, we're back to square one. We have nothing concrete on Nolan and we don't have much hope of stopping him."

"Hey," Cole said. "Don't give up. We often have setbacks in cases. Granted, this is a big one, but we'll overcome it."

She thought for a moment then nodded. "You're right. God is in control and He'll see us through this."

For once of late, Cole actually believed God had a hand in all this. Or at least he wanted to believe it. With so little to go on, it was going to take everything he had to bring Saunders to justice.

Alyssa got up from the table and moved away for a wider view of Cole and Derrick. She'd done her best to keep up with the brothers' rapid-fire conversation. But as they'd tossed out thoughts of how Nolan might have learned of Frank's deception and how to proceed, her neck started to ache from swinging back and forth between them.

Feeling unsettled again, she needed to do something normal. She looked around for something, anything that fit her regular routine. Her children's homework folders sat at the end of the table. She should have signed off on their homework and returned the folders to the teacher this morning. They'd receive a demerit for every day she didn't bring them back, and they didn't deserve to suffer because of what was going on.

She took a seat at the end of the table and pulled out Riley's papers.

"We'll just have to hope Carter can get the autopsy done in a timely manner," she heard Cole say.

She tuned him out and sifted through the pages, smiling over Riley's good grades. A bright red paper caught her attention. Not remembering any homework on bright paper, she pulled it free. The page was filled with letters cut from magazines and resembled the threat that accompanied the rock.

This is your last warning, Alyssa. Stop in-

vestigating or the people around you will get hurt.

"Oh no, he means the twins." She dropped the paper. It floated down the table and landed near Cole. "I should've found this yesterday. What if he hurts them?"

Cole looked at her. "What's wrong?"

She pointed at the warning. He picked it up and shared it with Derrick.

"Where was this?" Cole asked.

"In Riley's homework folder." She glanced at the clock. "Dani should be here by now. We have to call her and make sure the kids are fine."

"I'll do it." Derrick dug out his phone and lifted it to his ear while Alyssa held her breath. "She's not answering."

Alyssa shot to her feet. "Do something, Cole. Please, do something."

"Don't panic," he said, his tone comforting. "Dani's phone could be dead."

"Are you kidding?" Derrick came to the end of the table. "You and I might forget to charge our phones, but Dani would never let her phone die."

Cole glared at his bother. "Maybe she

doesn't have good reception. You know how bad it can be around here."

"We have to go to the school."

"Let's give it a few more minutes and try again," Cole suggested.

"No!" Alyssa shouted. "I have to make sure they're okay."

"This could be a trap to get you out into the open. Why don't we send Derrick?"

"They're my children, Cole. If you won't take me, I'll drive myself." She headed to the coatrack and slipped into her jacket.

"Fine, but Derrick is coming with us." Cole grabbed a notepad and pen. "Let me leave Dani a note in case she shows up here so she can call us."

Derrick joined Alyssa at the coats. "Hey, don't worry, Alyssa. Cole's right. Cell service is inconsistent out here."

Alyssa nodded, but the knot in her stomach tightened and didn't let up even when they were on the road. Cole drove, and she and Derrick were charged with watching for Dani's SUV along the route. Alyssa kept her focus glued to the vehicles they passed and prayed over and over for her children's safety. They soon turned onto the street for the school and Alyssa scanned the parked cars.

"There." She pointed ahead to the left in the nearly deserted parking lot. "Dani's car."

"Not good." Derrick shared a look with Cole that raised Alyssa's apprehension to panic mode.

Derrick hopped out before Cole came to a complete stop, and Alyssa was right behind him. She heard Cole's boots following. Though fearing what she would find in Dani's car, Alyssa couldn't look away.

Dani lay across the front seat, her hair matted with blood, but Alyssa saw her chest rise and fall—she was alive. Alyssa scanned the backseat for Brianna and Riley. When she found it empty, panic took hold of her every thought.

Derrick jerked on the handle before yelling, "Dani's inside, not moving. You have a key?"

"No key," Cole yelled back. "We'll have to break the window." He ran around the back of his vehicle and Alyssa heard him talking to a 911 operator on his phone.

Alyssa hated that Dani was hurt, but she

couldn't focus on anyone but her children. "Where are Riley and Bri? Where are they?" She thought she was screaming, but Cole didn't seem taken aback by her tone of voice as he joined them and handed a tire iron to Derrick.

Well, she was screaming inside anyway. "Maybe they're still in the school. I need to talk to their teacher." She ran across the street, and she heard Cole say goodbye to the operator as he pounded after her.

"Call me after you get the car open," he shouted back at Derrick.

She took a quick glance back. "No, Cole. Go make sure Dani is okay."

"This might be a trap. Derrick will take care of her." He put his hand on her elbow and drew her close to his side. She felt protected, but what about her kids? They weren't protected now. They were helpless children.

FIFTEEN

Cole and Alyssa hurried into the school. On his way past the office, Cole glanced inside and found it empty. Good. With school already dismissed, the staff had relaxed their vigil. That meant they wouldn't have to waste time checking in before gaining access to the teacher or having an irate secretary trailing them for an explanation.

At the twins' classroom door, he stepped in front of Alyssa. "Let me check out the room first. You'll do them no good if you're hurt."

She nodded reluctantly, and he slipped into the room. The young teacher was alone grading papers at her desk. "Can I help you?"

Though he'd rather do anything than let Alyssa find out her children weren't safely in their teacher's care, he stepped back for

Alyssa to enter. Her gaze traveled around the room and she rushed to the teacher's desk.

"The twins, Ms. Unger," Alyssa said, panic fully in control. "Where are they?"

Ms. Unger laughed. "Relax. It's okay. You're not in trouble for being late. They've been picked up already."

Blood drained from Alyssa's face, and she clutched the back of a chair. She opened her mouth to speak, but only a croak came out.

"Who picked them up?" Cole asked, fearing the answer.

"Nolan Saunders."

Alyssa's hand flew to her mouth and her chin dropped to her chest.

"Did I do something wrong, Mrs. Wells?" Ms. Unger got up and joined them. "You and he trade off picking up all the time." When Alyssa didn't reply, she added, "He's still authorized to pick them up, right? I mean, you didn't change that, did you?"

Cole swallowed past the stone in his throat. He couldn't believe he'd forgotten something as basic as informing the school that Saunders shouldn't be allowed to pick up the twins anymore. With Dani taking the kids back and forth, the issue simply hadn't crossed his mind. But now he could only blame himself for the lapse. Still, he couldn't stand to see Ms. Unger in such distress. "It's okay. She just thought she'd find them here," he said, keeping his tone light. "If he picked them up at the regular time, they should be at the house by now."

"He was punctual as usual, but I have to say the class was disappointed when he didn't drive up in his squad car and run his lights for them as he often does."

Cole slipped his hand under Alyssa's elbow. "We should get going."

She didn't respond, and he eased her toward the door.

"Is everything okay, Mrs. Wells?" Ms. Unger called after them.

"It's been a long day," Cole answered for Alyssa and escorted her out of the room.

"He has them, Cole," she said so quietly Cole had to strain to make out her words. "Nolan has them, and I don't know what to do." Her steps faltered and Cole wrapped an arm securely around her back to keep her from dropping to the floor.

Cole's heart ripped in two. He'd promised to care for her and her children and he'd let all of them down. He didn't think he could feel worse than he had the day Mac died, but he did. He'd made a promise, and didn't keep it.

He supported her all the way to the door. After making sure no one lurked outside, they exited the building and crossed the road. At the car, he saw Dani sitting and holding a gauze pad on her head and Derrick looking down on her with brotherly concern. Cole felt a brief flash of relief at Dani's recovery, but it floated quickly away.

"Are the twins inside?" Dani asked, but Cole could tell she didn't really expect them to be.

"Saunders picked them up," Cole said. "We should get back to the house and come up with a plan."

Derrick helped Dani from the car and Cole escorted Alyssa to his SUV.

"Any thoughts on where Nolan may have taken the kids?" Cole asked Alyssa.

"No. He's proved that I don't know him at all." She shivered under his arm. "They could be anywhere."

Cole pulled open the back door. "I'm so sorry I let him get to them."

"It's not your fault." She looked up at him, her eyes vacant. "It's mine. I should've remembered to remove him from the authorized pick-up list. Then he could never have done this."

"Don't do this to yourself, Alyssa." He squeezed her arm and told himself he should follow his own advice. Still, he knew he'd continue to blame himself until the twins were back in his care. Even then, he didn't know if he'd be able to let it go.

Looking at the night sky, Cole slammed the folder on the dining table. They had no leads. None. They no more knew where Saunders had taken the twins than they had six hours ago. At least Alyssa was no longer sitting in the chair, rocking herself back and forth until he thought she might wear a hole in the floor. After much persuading, he and Dani had finally convinced Alyssa to rest in her bedroom, though he doubted she was sleeping.

"We'll find them." Dani came up behind him and slipped an arm around his waist.

"I don't know how you can be so sure when we have no leads."

"We have a lot of irons in the fire. Something will pan out soon."

He rubbed his hand over his face and dropped onto a chair. "I screwed up big-time, Dani."

"Hey, I'm the one Saunders got the drop on."

"And I'm the one who didn't insist on the kids staying here. If anything happens to them…" His voice cracked with emotion.

Dani pulled out the chair next to him. "As much as I don't like what's happening, I do like the fact that you've finally let yourself feel something again. It's plain as day that you're head over heels in love with Alyssa."

He snapped his head up. "What?"

"You're in love with Alyssa. Otherwise you wouldn't be feeling this so deeply."

"You're way off base here, Dani. It's just guilt. Something I'm really good at feeling."

Dani smiled. "It's okay if you're not ready to admit it. But we all see it."

"All?" he asked not really wanting to know the answer.

"Derrick and I."

"The two of you have talked about this?"

"Of course. He's happy you've come back to life, too."

Cole shook his head and thought about the past few days. He *had* come to life. Opened his heart and hoped for more than the sad existence he'd been living. Was that thanks to Alyssa?

With the twins missing, it didn't matter. None of it. He may be in love with Alyssa, but he needed to keep his focus off himself right now. Only his full and complete attention on finding the twins would do. Or Saunders would make good on his threats and do something too horrific to bear.

Alyssa climbed out of the bed and paced the room. The walls seemed to close in on her. She was supposed to be resting, but how could she rest when Nolan had her babies? She really didn't think he planned to kill them, but then he'd proven the lengths he'd go to, hadn't he?

Her phone vibrated and she grabbed it from the dresser to look at the text message.

I have the twins. They're safe for now, but if you tell anyone about this message, they won't be. Call me at this number.

She thought about ignoring the warning and going to Cole, but she wouldn't risk her children's lives. Her heart beat hard enough to erupt from her chest as she dialed the number.

"Let me talk to them," she said as soon as Nolan answered.

"They're not with me," he quickly replied.

"What? Where are they? Who has them?"

"Relax. They're sound asleep and a friend is watching them."

Her heart lurched at the thought of someone else involved in Nolan's drug empire taking care of her children. "If you hurt them, Nolan, I swear I will make you pay."

He laughed at her much like he had in the past when he didn't think she could do something. "Nothing's going to happen to them if you do as I say."

She had no choice but to follow his directives. "Tell me what to do, and I'll do it."

"First, keep this between us. No running

to the other room and telling the Justice clan about this."

"You're watching us?"

"Of course. I'm right outside your window. I want you to climb out and join me."

Suddenly uncertain of what to do, she glanced at the window. "And then what?"

"Then we'll take a little drive, and once I'm sure the Justices aren't following us, you can call and tell them where the kids are."

She couldn't trust him to follow through. But what choice did she have? Her children's lives were at stake and she had to obey his directions. "I'll be right out."

"I don't want them tracking you by your phone so leave it in the room, Alyssa."

She disconnected and put her cell on the dresser. She dug out a warm sweater from her suitcase. After slipping into it, she opened the window and climbed out. A biting, cold wind pummeled her body and she lost her balance. When she recovered her footing, Nolan crept out of the shadows. He was holding his gun.

The full implication of what she'd done by joining Nolan out here hit her, and she raised her head to the dark night sky to offer a prayer.

"Close the window." Nolan pressed the gun into her back. "Quietly."

Be with us all, Lord, she thought then complied, slowly lowering the window down. Nolan grabbed her arm and dragged her across tall dunes. He hurried, his long strides moving quickly, and she struggled to keep up. Her shoes filled with sand and cold seeped through her sweater. They trudged for miles, and when she felt as if she couldn't go one more step, he made a sharp turn and hauled her up to the road. A four-door sedan she'd never seen Nolan drive was parked on the side of the road.

"A rental," he said, proving he knew what she was thinking.

They'd been good friends for so long. He knew her well and would be able to pre-empt any attempt she made to thwart him. He opened the driver's door and pushed her across the console before climbing in and turning on the heater. Once on the road, the warm air thawed her feet and hands, but her heart remained iced over.

He glanced at her, the glow from the dash casting an eerie green pallor to his face. "It feels good to have everything out in the open so we can talk honestly."

"You don't know what honest means." She crossed her arms and slid away from him.

"Hey, don't be that way." He paused, his eyes lifting to the rearview mirror, likely checking to see if anyone followed them. "I had to lie to you to protect you."

"Right. And is that what you're doing now? Protecting me by kidnapping my children?"

"Well, no," he said. "But that's your fault. If you hadn't spied on me like that and then hired the PIs to come after me, we'd be having a quiet night at home like we always do."

"Please. I didn't spy on you. I was just in the wrong place at the wrong time. Besides, you're the one selling drugs."

He looked at her long and hard before turning back to the road. "Seems to me that after being married to Todd, you'd be a little more understanding of why I need to make some extra cash."

"We might've needed money, but Todd would never stoop as low as you."

"I don't want to talk about Todd. This is about you and me. I did what I had to do so I could provide for you and the twins once we got married."

"Married!" She shot him a horrified look. "We were friends. Nothing more."

"For now, but we were getting so close that would've changed."

"No, it wouldn't, Nolan. You did all of this for nothing."

He glared at her, but the anger disappeared quickly and he smiled. "Not for nothing. You'll see. With Todd out of your life, you need a man to take care of you. I can be that man."

She didn't need any man. *Except Cole.* She forced the thought away. "So *was* Todd involved in all of this?"

"No. He couldn't see the beauty of our operation. He was too chicken to take a risk and make enough money to properly take care of you and the twins. It was just one more area where he failed you."

Her stomach churned in revulsion. "So you killed him."

He fixed a hard stare on her. "He threatened to report us. He had to be eliminated."

Eliminated. What a way to talk about another human being. How could she ever have thought Nolan was a good man?

She was thoroughly revolted and wanted to tell him so, but his razor-sharp glare told her to bite her tongue before he acted rashly. She looked out the window, watching miles of deserted beach fly by before he turned into a pricey beachfront neighborhood where homes sat far apart for privacy. He slowed and swung into the driveway of one of the rental properties she managed.

"What are we doing here?"

"Oh, right, you don't know how helpful your little career has been to me." He shifted into Park. "I've used your properties on and off for years to distribute my meth. It's worked out well. No one has suspected a thing."

"How could you use me like that and think I might fall in love with you?" She held up her hand. "Don't bother answering. There's nothing you could say to defend your actions."

"I wasn't using you, Alyssa. This is just

business. A business that can secure our future together if you'd let go of this high-and-mighty act." He put a hand on her arm, but she jerked free.

His logic was as full of holes as her heart. She'd once trusted him. Shared her hopes and dreams. Her failures and successes. And all that time he was using her for his own gain. She was such a bad judge of men.

When she and her children got out of here, she'd have to do a lot of soul-searching. She may not need a man in her life, but time spent with Cole showed her she still wanted a companion to share the trials and tribulations of life.

First, though, she had to survive this one.

"I got the DNA back on the cigarette," Kat announced over the speaker on Cole's phone.

"Speak up, Kat. It's hard to make out what you're saying."

"Sorry," she said louder. "We're in the car. We have a match for the DNA. He's a known drug dealer."

"Who is he?" Cole's adrenaline started to pump and he glanced from Dani to Derrick, both sitting across the dining table from him with their laptops open.

"Name is Lenard Gaddy," Kat went on. "He's a Pacific Bay resident. Served time for distribution of meth. He's also a suspect in a double homicide a few years ago."

Dani let out a low whistle, her fingers flying over her keyboard. "Name's not common. I should be able to track him down pretty easily."

"I have a last known address so that should help." Kat rattled off the address, and Cole jotted it down on a notepad.

"You just get this info or have you had a chance to research him?" Dani asked, still typing.

"I called the minute I got his particulars. Figured between you and Derrick we'd get the information faster."

"Glad you recognize my superiority in computer research," Dani said, laughing.

Kat snorted. "Puh-lease."

Cole liked seeing their good humor, but they had to focus to get the twins back alive. "Dani and Derrick, see what you can find on

Gaddy. I'll ask Alyssa if she knows anything about him."

"You're welcome." Kat's sarcasm came through the phone loud and clear.

"Sorry, Kit Kat." Cole stood. "You know I appreciate your help."

"Still doesn't hurt to hear it," she said, but her tone was lighthearted. "I've got a call in to my contacts at the Portland Police Bureau. I'll let you know if they have anything to add on Gaddy."

They quickly said their goodbyes, but Dani and Derrick didn't look up from their computers before Cole took off for the bedroom.

He stopped outside Alyssa's room and knocked on the door. He hated to wake her if she'd managed to fall asleep, but this lead was too good not to get her input.

She didn't answer so he knocked again. "Alyssa," he said. "I need to talk to you."

Time slipped by and he felt as if a countdown clock ticked away in his head.

"Alyssa," he said, louder this time.

When she failed to answer, he twisted the knob and found the door locked. He pounded on the door one more time with all his strength. If she was in there she had to hear him.

Panic rising, he shouted, "I'm coming in." He kicked the door. The wood fractured as the lock gave way. The door crashed into the wall and ricocheted back, slamming into his shoulder.

Ignoring the stinging pain, he rushed into the room and found it empty. A bolt of fear shot through his heart and he charged into the adjoining bathroom. No sign of Alyssa. His breath seemed to solidify in his throat.

"Where are you?" he said, back in her bedroom looking for any sign of her whereabouts.

Derrick joined him, his eyes going wide at the sight of the damaged door.

"Alyssa's missing," Cole said.

"There's her cell." Derrick pointed at the dresser.

Cole ran to it. "She wouldn't leave the house without her phone."

"Maybe she's in the kids' room," Derrick suggested.

Phone in hand, Cole was out of the room and across the hall in a flash, but the bedroom was empty, too. He unlocked her cell. "She got a text and then made a call about fifteen minutes ago. Neither number is assigned to a contact name."

"So it's not someone who calls her often."

"Dani can track the number." Running down the hall, he thumbed to the text message.

I have the twins. They're safe for now, but if you tell anyone about this message, they won't be. Call me at this number.

"It has to be Saunders." Cole barreled into the family room. "Alyssa's gone. I think she's gone to meet Saunders to save her kids." He held out the phone for Dani to see the text and number.

She clicked open a file on her computer. "Not Saunders's cell or home number, which isn't surprising. He knows enough to use an untraceable phone." She navigated to a reverse phone look-up page. "It's a prepaid cell."

Cole stifled a curse. "So how are we going to find her?"

"Maybe Gaddy will lead us to Saunders." Dani slid her computer to face Cole. "I managed to find Gaddy's phone info and hacked his account." Dani opened a map program and tapped her screen. "His GPS places him here. Interestingly enough, the property is a rental managed by Alyssa."

"This could be where Saunders has taken the kids and Alyssa." Cole turned for the door, but Derrick grabbed his arm. "Rushing in is a fool's game. Better to make a plan first."

Derrick was right. They were on the way to confront a killer. A killer who had the woman and children who were coming to mean a lot to him, and he wouldn't do anything to risk their lives. But he couldn't help thinking that every second they waited was another second in which he could lose the family he'd started to love.

SIXTEEN

Coming face-to-face with the man in Dani's photo, Alyssa shivered. He had a long, narrow, pockmarked face and full lips that turned down at the corners. His eyes were dark, almost black, and focused on Nolan. She shuddered in revulsion, and he turned to meet her gaze, his eyes suddenly filling with a prurient interest that left her nauseous.

How could Nolan leave Brianna and Riley with this creep?

"Take a hike, Gaddy," Nolan said to the guy. For a moment it seemed as if he might argue, then Nolan pointed his gun in Gaddy's direction. With a glare that sent fear into Alyssa's heart, Gaddy grabbed a worn jacket from the sofa and left. Nolan shoved his gun into his holster and locked the door before crossing to her.

"How could you leave the kids with him?" She let all of her fury loose by pounding on his chest.

He grabbed her wrists in an iron hold, pinching and bruising the skin. "Relax, sweetheart. I made sure they were asleep before I left and threatened him with his life if he touched them."

"I want to see them." She tried to pull her hands free, but his fingers held tight.

"No problem." He let go of one wrist but held fast to the other, dragging her down the hall to a bedroom. He gently opened the door. Her precious babies slept cuddled together in a large bed. She took a step toward them, but Nolan jerked her to a stop.

"You've seen enough." He hauled her back down the hallway and dropped her onto a worn flowery sofa. He stood looking down on her, his face a mass of confusion. "Don't you know how much I love your kids? I'd never do anything to hurt them." He dropped onto the sofa next to her and took her hands. "Marry me, Alyssa. I have enough money put away to last for years. We can run away together and be the family I've always dreamed of."

"I'm not going anywhere with you."

"But we have to. Don't you see?" He squeezed her hands. "A few men who wouldn't follow directions had to be silenced. I thought I'd covered my tracks, but the Astoria police chief is a former homicide detective, and he tracked me down on one of the cases. He's buddies with my dad and he'd been able to cover up my involvement until you and your PI got all nosy. The chief knew it was only a matter of time before you uncovered the evidence. He wasn't about to go to jail for obstruction, so he won't protect me anymore. That means I have to get out of town tonight, and I'm not leaving without you."

"I'd never go anywhere with a man like you." She jerked her hands free and ran for the hallway. If she could get to the kids, she could grab them and flee.

She heard Nolan's feet pounding on the tile floor behind her. She ran faster, panting like she had the other night when his men had chased her. She strained ahead to reach for the doorknob to the kids' bedroom. Her fingers touched the cool metal.

Just an inch more.

A hand shot out behind her and grabbed her hair. He jerked her back.

She swallowed her cry of pain so she wouldn't wake the twins, but a sob slipped out.

He turned her to face him, his eyes crazed and completely strange. "We *are* going away tonight, and we *are* getting married. Brianna and Riley *will* be mine. Got that?"

He jerked her hair again, wrenching her head back then pulling her closer until she was face-to-face with him. His sour breath fanned over her face and his eyes glazed over in that weird stare again.

He drew his gun and pressed the cold barrel against her temple. His eyes bore into hers, sending a chill down her spine. She looked away, but before she did, she saw he'd lost his sanity and she knew without a doubt if she didn't go along with his demands, he would kill her and her children.

Help me, Father. Please help me get away from Nolan and safely reunite me with my children.

Cole stood in the kitchen watching Saunders manhandle Alyssa. The man had clearly gone over the edge. Saunders kept his gun at her forehead and hauled her into a small living room, where he sat next to her on the sofa.

Fear as Cole had never known it raced through his body. He wanted to jump Saunders now, but with the gun pressed to Alyssa's head, Cole couldn't risk it. He could do only one thing. Pray.

Father, please. If You've ever heard me, hear me now. Keep Alyssa and the twins safe.

He slowly eased backward, wishing they'd arrived here before Saunders had drawn his gun. Freeing Alyssa now would be more difficult, but with Saunders facing away from the hallway, they could rescue the twins without being seen.

Cole slipped out the door and felt relief at seeing Derrick and Dani standing at the ready. He ignored the worried looks of his siblings and told them what he'd observed inside. "Alyssa would want us to make sure the kids are safe before doing anything else. So we get them out first."

"Agreed," Derrick said and Dani nodded.

"Okay, Dani, I need you in the car. Derrick by the back door. I'll go in, get the kids one at a time and hand them off to you, Derrick. You take them to the car." He fixed his eyes on Dani. "When you have both of them, you take off."

"I'm not leaving you two behind. Plus it'd be faster if we all go in—we can get them together and then leave together."

Cole shook his head. "We'd risk all of us being captured that way. Better there's only one person inside at a time in case things go south."

Dani frowned.

"It's the best plan to ensure their safety," Derrick added.

"After the kids are gone," Cole went on and faced Derrick, "I'll need you to create a diversion out front so I can jump Saunders without Alyssa getting hurt."

"Ringing the doorbell should bring Saunders to the door."

"Good. But you'll need to keep his attention to give me enough time to get Alyssa out of there."

"I can do that." Derrick grinned.

"So we have a plan?" Cole glanced at Dani, her brow still furrowed. "The kids need you, Dani. They know you and trust you."

"I still don't like leaving a man behind."

Cole got that. You never left a team member behind, but in this case, the lives of two children were at stake. "Can't be helped if we want to ensure the twins' safety. So we're good to go?"

Derrick nodded and Dani gave a clipped nod also. Cole waited for her to climb into his car, then he slipped inside the house. He heard Alyssa trying to calm Saunders down. Her soothing tone made Cole even angrier. If he'd protected her properly, she wouldn't be in a room with a killer much less be swallowing her fear to coo at him this way.

Cole felt like he might explode. He took a step in her direction, but a flashback of her bent over her children, her face alight with love for them, stopped him and he went down the dark hallway.

He opened the door Alyssa had tried to reach. He spotted the twins, and relief flooded through his body. Riley slept near the wall, Brianna near the edge of the bed. He slowly scooped her into his arms, careful not to wake her. He took slow measured steps down the hall to keep from jostling her, but her soft curls still moved with his steps. Outside, he gently settled her in Derrick's arms, but not before taking a long look at her peaceful face.

Cole wanted to smooth the hair from her eyes, but he didn't want to risk waking her. His heart constricted. Dani was right. He'd fallen in love, all right. He'd fallen for Alyssa and her kids—hook, line and sinker. All three of them had slipped into his heart and opened it, giving him a capacity for love he thought he'd never feel again.

"Okay?" Derrick asked, snapping Cole back to the mission.

"Get her to the car." Cole headed back inside, picked up Riley and hurried back down the hallway. Riley would be so mad when he found out he'd failed to protect and rescue Brianna. Cole would have a talk with the little man and help him realize he couldn't take care of her every moment of the day. No one could do that, least of all a young child.

So why was he trying to do the same thing? Trying to protect everyone he loved all the time was just as futile. His steps faltered for a moment before he caught his rhythm again and hurried out the door. He transferred Riley to Derrick's arms. "I'm going back in to assess the situation. I'll come out to update you before we proceed."

Derrick nodded and Cole drew his weapon before moving through the house again. Saunders and Alyssa still sat on the sofa, their backs to him. Saunders held his weapon in his hand, but instead of pressing it to her head, his arm rested along the back of the sofa.

Could Cole get to Alyssa faster than Saunders could shoot her? Probably. But not before Sanders snaked his arm around her throat and took her hostage again. Their plan of surprise was still the best plan.

Cole slipped outside again. Dani pulled his

car from the curb and Derrick stood nearby watching her leave. Relief over the twins' safety lightened his heart. When Derrick turned, Cole gave his brother a thumbs-up, telling him to head to the front door. Derrick moved up the sidewalk, and Cole returned to his position in the hallway.

Gun at the ready, Cole waited. The doorbell rang and Saunders responded by putting his gun to Alyssa's head just as Cole had known he'd try to do if Cole had jumped him before.

"Is that really necessary?" Alyssa said with a calm that impressed Cole. "It's probably that salesman we saw on the way in."

"What salesman?"

"Didn't you see him? He was carrying a black case." Cole couldn't help but smile in appreciation. Alyssa was so amazing, instinctively helping him and Derrick in their plan.

Saunders riveted his attention on her. He seemed to be trying to figure out if she was lying. He suddenly got up and dragged her by the wrist to the door. He pushed Alyssa against the wall behind him and approached the window in the door with caution. Cole moved closer and hoped Saunders would release Alyssa.

Saunders quickly glanced through the window, then flattened his body against the wall. Cole recognized the defensive maneuver. Saunders was afraid someone was going to open fire.

They stood there. Time ticking by.

The house was cold, but Cole felt perspiration trickle down his back. He thought about taking a shot at Saunders, but Cole wanted to end this situation without anyone getting hurt.

Saunders slowly moved to the window. Took a longer look and then flattened himself against the wall again. He repeated the pattern again and again, each glance out the window longer and longer until he stood staring outside.

The window fogged over. He released Alyssa's wrist and rubbed his fingers over the pane.

Cole waved at Alyssa. Their gazes met and relief filled her eyes for a moment before terror reclaimed them. His heart constricted, but he forced himself to stay calm and send her signals that said on the count of three to run toward him.

He inched closer, dropping one finger at a time, his focus on Saunders, who hadn't moved. When Cole let the last finger fall, he was close enough for Alyssa to move behind him. They eased back. One step at a time. Silently.

"Something's wrong," Saunders said and suddenly spun. "What the—"

Knowing his plan to move Alyssa out of the room before anyone got hurt was lost, Cole centered Alyssa behind him. She clung to the sides of his Kevlar vest. Saunders reacted in a flash, sighting his weapon and getting off a shot. The bullet sliced through Cole's arm. His instincts kicked in and he didn't hesitate but fired off two rounds center mass as he'd been taught in his marshal's training.

Saunders went down.

"Get out of here, Alyssa," Cole called out and rushed to Saunders. Cole couldn't risk looking back to see if she listened, but he didn't hear movement.

He kicked Saunders's weapon away from his body. Cole knelt by Saunders and felt for a pulse. Found none. Resigned, he sat back and checked his arm. Just a flesh wound, barely even bleeding. He spotted Alyssa standing mouth open, eyes glassy and exhibiting signs of shock.

As regret ate at him for not finding another way out of this without ending a life, Cole went to her. Her whole body trembled, and he drew her into his arms, but she pushed free.

"Brianna and Riley," she said, turning away.

"We already took care of them. They're with Dani and are probably at the beach house by now."

Gun outstretched, Derrick came into the room, his gaze going to Saunders's lifeless body then to Cole. Cole shook his head to let Derrick know Saunders didn't make it.

"You call this in?" Derrick asked.

Cole shook his head. "We need to get Carter over here before making an official call to the local authorities."

Alyssa started crying, and Cole took her into his arms again, pressing her head to his chest. He inhaled her soft flowery scent and lifted his head.

Thank You, Father. For being here. For hearing my prayers. Thank You, thank You, thank You for protecting Alyssa and the twins.

Even with Cole's arm around her and the heat blasting from the car's heater, Alyssa couldn't quit shaking. Thank God Cole's gunshot wound only required a few stitches. She moved closer to him and stared at the back of Kat's head. Dani had arrived home with the twins and found the other two Justice siblings, Kat and Ethan, waiting at the beach house. Once they'd learned Gaddy's identity, they hopped on a helicopter in case their siblings needed help.

What a family. Rescuers, every one of them. They'd fulfilled their promises by keeping all of them safe and ending this terrible ordeal with Nolan. Not in the way she'd thought it would end, but at least their nightmare was over.

She turned to Cole and found the same brooding look that had creased his face since she'd recovered enough from the shock to notice. "You had to shoot him."

"I know. That still doesn't make it any easier to take."

She took his hand. "I'm alive because you chose to do the difficult thing."

His expression softened, and he traced the side of her face with a gentle finger. "That's the only thing that's making this bearable at the moment."

She looked into his eyes, getting lost. He moved closer. She knew he was going to kiss her. Could almost taste his lips on hers. She waited as he inched closer, feeling his breath soft on her face. One last look and his lips claimed hers. Thrilled to be alive, thrilled to be with him, she forgot all her reservations about him and responded. He slipped his arms around her and pulled her closer.

Time ceased to exist and she knew happiness she never thought she'd experience again.

"Ahem." Kat loudly cleared her throat. "I said we're here."

Cole's head lifted and Alyssa tried to pull out of his embrace, but he kept his arms locked around her. "Something you need to know about this family," he whispered.

"There's no privacy. None." He smiled down on her. "Trust me. I know."

Breathless, Alyssa willed her thundering heart to slow.

What was she thinking letting Cole kiss her like that? Had she already given her heart to a man she still wasn't sure she knew?

SEVENTEEN

Alyssa kissed Riley's forehead then moved across the bedroom to Brianna and brushed her hair back. She pressed her lips against the warm forehead of her daughter and sighed.

Thank You, Father, for protecting my babies. And thank You for bringing the Justice family into my life. You have truly provided and I am forever grateful.

She'd have to tell them about Nolan's death tomorrow, but once they got through that, their life could go back to normal. Well, sort of normal. After everything that had happened with Nolan, she couldn't go back to the duplex to live, so she'd have to find an inexpensive apartment. Cole had already offered to let them stay at the rental until she could find a place.

She got up and took one last lingering look.

She smiled, closed the door and headed down the long hallway. She found the Justice family sitting around the long oak dining table. Except for Dani and Derrick, they were all so different. She took the time to study the two siblings she'd met just hours ago in the chaos. Ethan sat at the head of the table, a serious expression on his face. Kat sat on the other end, face lit by laughter, her petite body nearly dwarfed by the large table.

Cole faced Alyssa, and his eyes met hers. All the emotions that zinged between them in the car were once again visible on his face. She should want to pull away, but it was getting harder and harder to resist him. When the others turned to look at her, she snapped her gaze free and felt her face heat up under their scrutiny as she crossed the room.

"How are the twins doing?" Dani asked.

"Fine." Alyssa sat next to Cole in the only vacant chair. "I wanted to say thank you again to all of you. I don't know what would've happened without you." A shiver claimed her body and Cole reached out to hold her hand.

Eyebrows all around the table went up, and Alyssa slowly pulled her hand away.

"So I guess now that you have everything under control, Kat and I'll be shoving off in the morning." Ethan arched an eyebrow at Cole. "Would be good if you released Derrick, too, so we can get caught up on background checks."

"Derrick's good to go, but," Cole paused and turned toward Dani, "could you stay for another day or so? I have a few things I need you to do."

Dani cast a questioning look at her brother but nodded.

"Before you all leave, I wanted to talk to you about Todd," Alyssa said. Feeling nervous asking them for anything more after all they'd done for her, she clutched her hands under the table. "When I was with Nolan, he admitted Todd had nothing to do with the drug business. In fact, he was killed because he was going to report Nolan. I realize Nolan telling me this doesn't do anything to clear Todd's name. So can anyone think of a way to do so?"

Cole swiveled toward Alyssa. "Agent Carter's

already planning a thorough investigation of the entire Pacific Bay Police Department. I also asked him to get permission from his supervisor to reopen Todd's case."

"Great," Alyssa said, but she'd hoped Cole and his siblings would want to investigate, too. If anyone could clear Todd's name, it would be the Justice family. *And Cole would have to stay in Pacific Bay,* she thought but pushed it away.

"As a sworn officer of the law, Carter will have the best chance to get the ruling on Todd's case reversed." Cole took her hand under the table. "But don't worry. If he doesn't find anything, we'll investigate and make sure Todd's name is cleared." He squeezed her hand and smiled.

Alyssa could get lost in that smile, wanted to get lost in it, but after a long moment, she pulled away. Now that all the excitement was over, she wasn't sure where they stood. She knew she had feelings for Cole, but how did he feel about her? Was he ready for a relationship? Was she? And would they have a chance to figure it out before he left Pacific Bay behind?'

* * *

Cole couldn't sleep so he paced in front of the big window in the family room. He didn't need to worry about Alyssa and the twins any longer, but he couldn't put away his frustration of failing her. If only he hadn't allowed Saunders to get near them. Then he'd know he was in control and could declare his love for her and the twins.

Why, Father? Why make this so difficult?

"Thought I heard someone out here." Dani padded into the room in bare feet. She tucked her bathrobe tighter and wrapped her arms around her middle. "Seemed like things were good with you earlier, so why the frown?"

He shrugged.

"Does this have something to do with why you want me to stay?"

"Kind of." He looked into the dark of night. "Alyssa will be staying here while she finds an apartment. I thought it might be good if you were here to help her out."

"Translated—you want a buffer between you two." She stepped in front of him. "Since you clearly have a thing for each other, why do you need a buffer?"

"I won't waste time denying I've fallen for her. I have. Hard. But I'm the wrong person for her and I can't seem to remember that when she's around."

"Care to tell me why you're so wrong for her?"

He didn't want to, but maybe talking about it would help. "She doesn't want to be married to a guy with a dangerous job."

Dani's perfectly plucked brow rose. "And she told you this?"

"Not in so many words, but yeah, she said that she had a hard time with Todd being in the line of danger."

"It's not like you're a marshal anymore. You aren't in danger all that often, Cole."

"But still."

She rested her hands on his shoulders. "It sounds to me like you're trying to come up with an excuse not to have to face the real problem."

He hated that she could see through him, but she'd always been able to do so. "I guess you've noticed that after losing Mac, I've developed this thing about protecting others."

"A 'thing' is putting it mildly, but yeah we

all know that you feel guilty about surviving when Mac died."

"I keep getting reminders about how that can happen again. The most recent one was tonight when Saunders took Alyssa and the twins." He shook his head. "I couldn't live with myself if anyone else I'm responsible for gets hurt."

"You're my big brother and I respect you more than you know, Cole, but that's foolish thinking." Her tone had hardened. "We can't control things around us. Not a single one of us can. God is in charge. He decides on life-and-death issues. If your line of thinking is right, then not a single person in this world should risk loving others. Do you think that's how we all should live? Should Kat and Mitch not get married? Should Ethan and Jennie get divorced?"

"No, of course not. They deserve to be happy."

"And so do you. Stop setting rules for yourself that you can't possibly keep. God intended for us to share our lives with others. And He didn't mean for us to live in fear that they will be taken from us."

Cole studied his baby sister. She was so wise at times that he forgot how young she was. She'd always been able to embrace her faith and live it—and life—fully.

He took her in his arms and hugged her hard. "You're the best sister a guy could ask for."

"And don't you forget it, Cole Justice." She laughed, and his heart lit with joy that had been a long time in coming.

Cole headed up the walk to his rental house after dropping off the twins at school. He unlocked the door and let Alyssa go in first. After his discussion with Dani last night, he'd been thinking about a future with Alyssa. His mind kept coming back to the fact that she didn't want to be married to someone who risked his life. Would he lay his feelings out there only for her to tell him she didn't want the kind of life he could give her?

There was only one way to find out. Ask her. But she'd been occupied all morning and the drive home from school was the first time they'd been alone. He didn't want to have such an important discussion without being able to look at her, so he'd waited.

She dropped her purse on the kitchen counter.

Cole stood in front of her so she couldn't move away from him. "Can I ask you something?"

"Sounds serious," she replied and leaned against the counter.

He shrugged. "I wondered how you knew when your marriage wasn't going to work anymore."

She flashed him a surprised look. "Actually, I'd hoped we would work things out until the day Todd died."

It was Cole's turn for surprise. "But you said you'd split up."

"We did, but I promised if he sought counseling to get over his anger issues we could give it another try. In hindsight, I can see I was being naïve. After he hit me I don't think I could've trusted him not to do it again." She sighed out a deep breath. "Besides, he'd changed so much by then, he wasn't the man I married anymore."

"Unfortunately, it's not uncommon for men

and women to change under the stresses of a law enforcement or military career."

She nodded. "I've seen it happen with some of our friends. But, honestly, I think Todd would've had the same crisis in any career he was in. I don't really blame the job."

"So you wouldn't be opposed to being married to a law enforcement officer again?"

Her eyes flashed up to his. "If I loved a man enough, I wouldn't care what he did for a living." She smiled. "He could even be a crazy PI like the men in your family and I wouldn't care. I'd be concerned for his safety, but finding love is too rare. I wouldn't let a job stand in my way."

Relief flowed through his body and he knew Dani was right. He'd been letting himself think Alyssa would bail on him the way Laura had so he wouldn't have to face his own issues. But Alyssa wouldn't bail on him or send him a Dear John email. She'd stuck by a man who didn't deserve it and even gave him a second chance. She wouldn't run from anything in a relationship. Maybe not even Cole's problems from the past.

Cole looked into her eyes, deeply, intently,

wanting to let go of everything and love this amazing woman. "You're really a special person."

"So are you," she said, letting out a long breath but not pulling away.

He wanted to kiss her. Was going to kiss her. But not like the last time. Then the joy of being alive had made them rush into it. Now he'd take his time. He put his hands on her shoulders then ran them down her arms. She shivered and he reveled in the effect his touch had on her.

He slipped his hands around her waist and drew her closer. She raised up on tiptoes as if urging him to kiss her. He held her with one arm and traced her lips with his finger. She closed her eyes and let out another breath.

"Look at me, Alyssa," he whispered.

Her eyes flashed open.

"I want to kiss you," he said.

She laughed and snaked her arms around his neck. "So what are you waiting for?"

Indeed, what was he waiting for? He slipped a wayward strand of hair behind her ear, his thumb brushing her temple. The temple Saunders had held a gun against less than twelve hours ago. Fear as terrifying as the day the IED took Mac out snaked through his heart. He couldn't breathe.

Dani was wrong. He couldn't do this.

He stepped back and took her arms from around his neck. Looked at her wrists bruised and raw from Saunders's manhandling. "I want a relationship with you so badly, but I can't. I just can't do this right now."

Her face exploded with pain, and he knew he'd blown it with her. Maybe forever. But no matter how much he loved her, and he did love her, he wouldn't kiss her again until he could tell her how much he cared. He only hoped she'd still be there when he finally succeeded in wrestling with his problems.

The twins were laughing with Dani when they got home from school, but Alyssa hadn't recovered from the abrupt end to what she had known was going to be the best kiss of her life so she didn't join in. Despite her best attempt to guard her heart, she'd fallen for Cole. Worse than that, she'd almost told him. But now…now she felt crushed. She'd found a man she could trust—but he couldn't trust himself. Until he learned to move past that, they couldn't be together.

She wished she was strong enough to go back to the duplex to get away from him. Or go to a hotel, but she couldn't afford it. She'd ask him to watch the twins tomorrow and she would spend the entire day finding an apartment with immediate occupancy. It would be best for all of them to simply say their goodbyes.

"Hey, Mom, the sun's out. Can we play outside?" Riley dropped his backpack in the middle of the floor. Brianna gently settled hers on the table.

"You know better than that, Riley." Alyssa gestured to pick up the bag.

"Sorry." He grabbed the backpack and set it on the table. "It's just, I thought maybe Cole might play football with me."

"That's up to Cole," she answered, hoping he'd say yes so he'd go outside and she wouldn't have to watch him brood.

Riley crossed the room to where Cole stood by the window and looked expectantly up at him. "You want to?"

"Are you kidding? Of course I do." He held out his fist and bumped Riley's.

"Snack first," Alyssa warned.

"Aw, Mom."

"Hey." Cole grabbed Riley and knuckled his head. "If you don't eat something you'll never stand a chance at beating me out there."

"Fine, but hurry, Mom, okay?"

She smiled at her son and went to the kitchen. She heard multiple sets of footsteps follow, and when she turned from getting yogurt from the refrigerator she found Dani leaning on the counter and Riley already on a bar stool.

"You have to wash your hands, Riley." He raced off to the bathroom.

Alyssa looked for Brianna and found her pulling a piece of paper from her backpack before shyly approaching Cole. She tugged on the back of his shirt, and he slowly turned.

"Hey, Brianna," he said softly.

"I made this for you. It's us. We're playing Pretty Pretty Princess." She handed the paper to him, and he studied it for a long moment. Alyssa could tell the picture moved him. He squatted to Brianna's level and smiled. "It's beautiful. Maybe we can play for real later."

Alyssa's heart was melting into a puddle, and she wished she could see her daughter's reaction.

"When I was little, my mom put all her favorite pictures on the front of the refrigerator," Cole went on. "I think something this special should have a place of honor there, don't you?"

She nodded and Cole gently scooped her up with his free arm. She settled her arm around his neck, and they came into the kitchen.

"Thank you," Alyssa mouthed as they passed.

Cole responded with a sweet smile that sent her heart thumping again. She couldn't keep wishing for things he couldn't give her. She busied herself with getting silverware and napkins out so she wouldn't think about it.

"How about we get washed up for a snack, too?" Cole asked after putting the picture under magnets from local businesses.

"Yes, please."

Cole took Briana to the kitchen sink and together they washed hands. Brianna giggled in a way Alyssa hadn't heard since Todd had moved out of their house. Alyssa set places for Riley and Brianna, and Cole came around the counter to sit. Instead of putting Brianna on the stool next to him as Alyssa figured he'd do, he settled her on his lap.

Riley charged up to them and gave Cole a suspicious look. "Where's Cole's yogurt? He needs a snack, too."

"Yeah, I need a snack, too." Cole smiled up at her again, his happiness in such direct contrast to the broken man she'd seen only moments ago that she simply stared back.

Dani cleared her throat. "Um, since the two of you seem so busy, I'll get the yogurt."

Alyssa felt her face flush red and was grateful when Cole looked away. Riley saved her by starting to chat about his day. Brianna chimed in every so often, but mostly she kept looking at Cole in a way that Alyssa hated to admit she herself had probably been doing. In fact, Brianna was so absorbed in watching him she barely touched her yogurt. When Riley finished and hopped down, she'd only taken a few bites.

Riley danced in place. "C'mon, Cole, let's go before it starts raining again."

"Get the football from the closet, and I'll be right there." Cole tweaked Brianna's nose. "Sorry, honey, it's time for me to go outside with Riley."

Brianna slipped off Cole's lap, her happiness evaporating in a puff. Cole got up and paused to stroke the back of Brianna's head for a few moments. He was an intuitive man, willing to help Brianna with her hurt feelings. After grabbing some water bottles from the fridge, he and Riley headed outside.

"Okay, so what's going on here?" Dani said the moment the door closed.

Alyssa worked on putting a blank expression on her face. When she thought she'd mastered it, she turned to Dani. "What do you mean?"

Dani laughed. "Good one. Like I could miss the tension in the air."

Alyssa cut her eyes at Brianna, who fixed her attention on them. "Big ears."

"Okay, later, but there *will* be a time for us to talk." Dani grabbed a soda from the fridge and with a meaningful glance left the kitchen.

"Eat up, sweetie," Alyssa said to Brianna. After checking to see that Dani had gone to her room, Alyssa went into the family room to watch Cole and Riley through the window.

Riley ran in circles and Cole chased, grabbing him and tackling him to the sand. Cole's back still must be hurting from the explosion and his gunshot wound, yet he didn't seem to care. Riley, eyes alight with laughter, climbed on top of Cole's chest and pinned him to the ground. Cole seemed to struggle for a while then, circling an arm around Riley, he came to his feet and swung Riley in a circle.

Alyssa could hear them both laugh through the window and their joy brought a smile to her face. Her children had been through so much, but Cole gave her hope that they really were resilient and would be okay.

Brianna joined her and looked longingly at the roughhousing pair. Her daughter didn't play outside much. She was more of a solitary books and movie kind of girl, but today she wanted to join in.

"You want to go out and play with them?" Alyssa asked.

"Cole didn't ask me." Her lip jutted out.

"I'm sure that's because he knew you had to finish your snack first. I'll bet he'd like it if you joined them."

She took a step then hesitated.

"It's okay, sweetie. You can go."

She took one last look at Alyssa then ran for her coat and out the door. Once outside, she slowly approached the pair. They didn't notice her at first, and she settled onto the dune. Cole spun around and when his eyes landed on her, he smiled widely and went to her. He knelt by her as Riley climbed onto his back. Alyssa expected him to wince, but he simply smiled down at Brianna and talked to her. She nodded and jumped up so fast it startled Alyssa. He flipped Riley to the front, said something to him and put him down. Riley ran toward the ball and Cole scooped Brianna into his arms.

Alyssa held her breath, waiting for her daughter to cry. She was much more fragile than Riley. Alyssa took a step toward the door to tell Cole to take it easy. But she didn't need to say anything. He swung her in circles as he had with Riley, but he cradled her gently in his arms instead of letting her fly.

Riley came over and tackled Cole's legs. He fell to the ground but landed on his side, protecting Brianna from the fall. She squealed in delight. Both of her children climbed on top of Cole.

They played that way until Cole called a truce and offered water to her children. Cole sat, legs outstretched, ankles crossed and Riley plopped down next to him, checking out Cole and mimicking his position.

Alyssa sighed and leaned her head against the window. Riley was desperate for a good male role model, and she certainly wanted one in his life. Someone strong, kind and ethical. Someone like Cole Justice.

How she'd ever thought he was like Todd was beyond her. True, Cole had withdrawn from life over his trauma in Iraq, but unlike Todd, Cole could interact with her children. He'd come through a life-altering experience, suffered from it, yet inside he wasn't cold and hard. Cole was warm and caring. The very opposite of Todd.

This thought should make her feel better, but the reverse was true. It took all of her reasons for not loving Cole out of the equation.

Now all that was left was to overcome Cole's problems—and she didn't even know where to begin.

EIGHTEEN

"You're sure about this?" Cole stared at Agent Carter. They'd just finished dinner when he'd summoned Cole to his hotel room to share information about the investigation that he wouldn't discuss on the phone. Cole couldn't imagine Carter had uncovered much in the first day of investigation, but Carter had proved Cole wrong.

"Positive," Carter said. "We picked up Gaddy, and he cut a deal by telling us everything he knows about the Saunders family. Turns out Chief Saunders was warned by the Astoria chief that we had proof of Nolan purchasing the suitcase. Chief Saunders in turn warned his son to flee."

Cole hated that two more cops would be implicated in this, but if both police chiefs had broken the law, they needed to pay. "So you'll be bringing Chief Saunders up on charges for obstructing justice."

Carter shifted in his chair. "Yes, but there's more. You may want to be sitting down for this."

Cole's gut tightened but he stood his ground. "Go on."

"We've uncovered proof that Nolan wasn't the head of the drug organization."

"Interesting. But not surprising enough to have to sit down."

"It's the top dog's identity that'll get to you."

"Out with it already," Cole snapped, getting tired of all of this drama.

"Nolan took his orders from his father."

"Chief Saunders?"

"Chief Saunders."

Cole let the news sink in. "So if Chief Saunders was in charge…"

"Then he could be the one who ordered Todd's murder. And maybe he ordered Alyssa's, too, while his son tried to warn her off."

"Then she's still in danger." And she needed protection. Cole's protection. Now!

"I've gotta go." He bolted for the door and

charged to his car. His heart racing, he revved the engine and dialed Dani.

"Hey, Cole," she answered.

"Where's Alyssa?" He shifted into drive and careened his car onto the street.

"She went for a run, why?"

"Chief Saunders is the real mastermind of the drug operation. He's the one who wants her dead."

"Oh, no," Dani said, letting her voice fall off.

"I need you to stay with the twins, and I'll find her." His mind raced with thoughts of Alyssa in the dark with no protection. "Did she say where she was going to run?"

"No. Oh, Cole. I'm so sorry. I should've asked but she seemed preoccupied and I didn't want to intrude."

"It's not your fault. You didn't think she was in any danger." *It's my fault,* his mind screamed. "I'll try calling her."

He ended his call and speed dialed Alyssa. The call went to voice mail. He slammed a fist on the steering wheel. "Think," he mumbled. "Where would she be?"

She'd told him she ran on the beach in the

morning and on the path at night. He'd try the path first. He wove in and out of the light evening traffic, praying he wasn't stopped for speeding.

Help me find her, Father. Please.

He turned into the parking lot and came to a screeching stop, then flew from the car to the jogging trail. A heavy chain was strung across the mouth of the trail announcing its closure due to a rockslide.

Cole's heart fractured. He'd chosen wrong. So wrong.

He reversed course and shot his SUV onto the highway. He cut off a car and their brakes squealed to a stop, the car nearly taking Cole out. He needed to relax. He couldn't help Alyssa if he was hurt in a car accident.

This couldn't be happening. He couldn't be late again. Not again.

"Father, please, please let me arrive on time," he whispered as he honked his horn at a slow-moving car then swerved around him.

He pressed the gas pedal, flying above the speed limit to get to the woman who'd captured his heart. So what if he had baggage from the past? Everyone did, but he'd wallowed in it long enough. It was time to move on. Live fully again. Declare his love for Alyssa and ask her to take him, baggage and all.

If she didn't come to any harm.

Lord, please. I can't lose Alyssa. Not now.

Alyssa's teeth rattled, her body a mass of shivers as she looked longingly at the sand. She'd been so busy concentrating on her rhythm as she ran to keep her mind off Cole that she hadn't heard Chief Saunders sneak up behind her on the beach. He'd pressed a gun into her back and forced her into the water. She'd been in the icy waves too long already, and she could feel her heart slowing down. She'd lived near the ocean long enough to know she'd soon get sleepy and then so relaxed that she'd slip below the tides to a watery grave. Just as Saunders hoped would happen.

She could handle dying—she really could. She knew her eternal resting place. But her children couldn't handle losing their only parent.

Oh, Lord, please don't let me die and leave my children without both parents.

Her eyes grew heavy, and she let her head fall back into the freezing surf. With her parents gone and no siblings, who would look after Riley and Brianna? A picture of Cole playing with them this afternoon, his eyes filled with the same mischief as her children, flashed into her brain.

Cole would be the perfect person to take them. The thought came unbidden to the surface. She trusted him. Fully, completely. He was gentle yet firm with the twins, and they'd already come to care for him. As had she. And now she may never get the chance to tell him how much she loved him.

The will to live took hold, and she slapped her hands against her arms to stay awake.

Heavenly Father, please send help. I want to live. How I want to live and make a life with Cole and my children.

Cole raced down the beach toward the rock where he'd first met Alyssa. His feet battled through the soft sand, slowing him down. He spotted a tall man standing near the shore, his back to Cole. He wore a uniform. Cole felt sure it was Chief Saunders, but he saw no sign of Alyssa.

"Please," he heard her say from the other side of the man. Cole craned his neck and caught sight of her in the water, submerged up to her chin. "My children need me."

"You should've thought of that before you let your boyfriend kill my son." The chief waved his gun. "Death will come sooner if you relax." The chief laughed. "It worked with Gibson and it'll work with you. When your body washes up, I'll make sure everyone thinks you felt so guilty over Nolan's death that you ended your life."

So that was his plan.

"No one will believe that. Especially not Cole. He'll come after you." Her words were slurred, and Cole knew from his military training that she was fast heading toward hypothermia.

If only he hadn't gone to the trail first. Now he could lose her.

Stop it, he warned himself.

He acted with the knowledge he had at the time, and that was all he could've done. Only God knew what was going to happen and Cole could finally live with that. But that didn't mean he wouldn't do everything within his power to save her.

He searched the beach for a way out of this disaster. If he drew the chief's attention, Alyssa could climb out of the water.

"Saunders," Cole shouted.

The chief spun. "Well, well, well. I couldn't have planned this better if I had scripted it myself. Now I can get rid of you both at the same time."

"Come on," Cole said. "You're a sworn officer of the law. Nolan wouldn't want you to kill on his behalf."

The chief snorted. "Fat lot you know. I've cleaned up that boy's messes too many times to count."

Was he saying he'd done the killing, not Nolan?

"I don't understand," Cole said and saw Alyssa rising out of the water behind the chief. She swayed but slowly moved toward the beach.

"Nolan was my son and I loved him dearly, but he could no more end someone's life than he could be the man I wanted him to be." He shook his head. "I wouldn't be here right now if he'd gotten rid of Alyssa like I told him. But no, he had to keep warning her, thinking he could scare her off and I would let her go."

"But you would've still killed her, right?" Cole dragged his eyes from Alyssa to keep from tipping off the chief.

"Of course I woulda. I haven't succeeded in the meth business for ten years by leaving loose ends."

"So the man in Astoria and Todd? If that wasn't Nolan's doing, why'd he tell everyone it was?"

"Was the only way to keep our men in line." The chief snarled. "Enough of this chitchat. I'm here to avenge Nolan's death. You messed with the wrong man, Justice." He continued rambling, but Cole tuned him out and focused on Alyssa.

She eased closer and signaled her intent

to ram the chief. Cole wanted to shake his head, tell her to back off. She was too weak and the chief was a big man. But she moved forward, her focus fixed on the chief, a pit-bull expression planted on her face.

As she took the last step, Cole made ready to hit the dirt. He wore his vest, but a stray bullet from the chief's gun could take him down.

Alyssa crossed her arms over her chest and plunged forward. Surprise flashed across the chief's face and his finger constricted on the trigger, but he was already on his way down when the gun exploded in a deafening bang. The bullet pierced a dune, sand spraying into the air.

Alyssa fell to the ground and didn't move.

Cole wanted to rush to her, but he had to subdue the chief while he was down. Cole dove onto the chief's back, knocking the gun away and forcing his face into the sand. Cole jerked the burly man's arms behind his back.

"Alyssa," Cole called out.

"Cole." Her weak voice gave him a moment's pause.

He had to restrain the chief and get her to the car to warm her body. Cole snagged handcuffs from the chief's belt and fastened them tightly.

"Take it easy, man," the chief growled.

Cole searched him, removing his backup weapon and Taser. Cole jumped up and scooped Alyssa into his arms. He cradled her against his chest, willing her to take whatever warmth she could from his body. "Hang in there, sweetheart. Don't leave me now. I love you."

"Love you, too." The words slipped out so quietly Cole wasn't certain he'd heard them.

"Get up," he yelled at the chief and drew his weapon.

The chief struggled to his feet.

"March," Cole barked and jabbed his weapon in the chief's back. He pressed hard, forcing him to move faster than he wanted.

In the light of the parking lot, Cole could see Alyssa's eyes were closed, her face pale and her lips blue. Stifling a curse, he found the chief's keys and locked his cuffs around a spoke in the wheel. He opened the passenger door and sat down, cradling Alyssa on his lap. He started the car, and cranked up the heat. Holding her shivering body close to his, he called for an ambulance and lifted his head in prayer to plead for her life.

Alyssa opened her eyes, but bright lights forced them closed again. Her body tingled and burned, the ache as reassuring as it was painful. She'd survived the water. The cold. Thanks to Cole. He'd protected her like he'd promised he would.

She opened her eyes again, squinting until they adjusted to the light. He stood near the window, his back to her. The sight of his broad shoulders reminded her that she could trust him to be there for her and her children. Not just tonight. Not only tomorrow. Always.

He turned and their eyes met. He didn't move. Not a muscle, but the love he declared at the beach shone on his face. She needed to touch him to be sure he was real.

"Mind coming a little closer?" she asked.

His lips tipped in that cute lopsided grin,

and her heart kicked into high gear as he slowly crossed the room.

He gently sat on the side of the hospital bed and pulled her hands out from under the warming blanket. He sandwiched them between his. "I'm sorry for not being there when you needed me."

"You were there. Every moment. Not physically at first, but thoughts of you gave me the strength to fight the cold."

He let her hands go and smoothed her hair back to study her. "I'm not sure if you heard me at the beach or not, but I love you." He declared his love so shyly that her heart melted.

"I love you, too."

His smile returned, wide and brilliant. "Does this mean you'd consider going on a date with me when you get out of here?"

"Just one date?"

"I didn't want to overwhelm you."

"You're not at all. I trust you, Cole. Completely and totally."

"Even with all of my issues from Iraq?"

"Actually, that's why I can trust you. You've been through so much and you still have a wonderful heart. If that experience didn't make it die, nothing will."

He trailed a finger down her cheek and along her chin. She twined her arms around his neck and pulled him closer. "I don't normally kiss on the first date—or, in this case, before the first date—but I don't think I can wait any longer."

His eyes caught fire before he closed them and settled his lips on hers. She returned his kiss with all the love she felt. She knew this was the perfect match for her. Only God could have taken two people with such baggage and made them whole enough to love again.

She vaguely heard the door open and a woman clear her throat. Cole lifted his head, regret coloring his expression. "Has anyone told you your timing stinks, Dani?"

"Nope," she said feigning innocence as she approached. "Riley and Brianna are outside waiting to see you."

"Thanks for bringing them and for taking care of them all the time."

"No problem. I kinda like the little squirts."

But Alyssa couldn't impose on her anymore. "Has the doctor mentioned when I can leave?"

"They want to keep you overnight," Cole answered.

"If you'll get my phone, I'll call one of my friends to keep them tonight."

"I don't mind watching them," Dani said.

Cole's eyes clouded over, and he looked at his sister. "Can you excuse us for a minute?"

Alyssa didn't know what she'd said, but Cole clearly didn't like it.

"You said you trusted me, right?" Cole said the minute the door closed.

"Yes."

"But not enough to take care of Riley and Bri?"

"What? No. I'd be thrilled if you wanted to take care of them tonight. I just didn't want to impose."

"Your children are not an imposition. They're part of you." He clutched her hands again. "I don't want to scare you by rushing things, but I've really come to care for them and can't imagine my future without them or you."

"You're not scaring me." She stroked the side of his face. "Far from it."

"Then it's settled. I'll take them home tonight and spoil them like crazy."

"Hey now," she laughed. "No one said anything about spoiling."

He laughed with her and she felt her heart fill with happiness. Finally she had everything she'd wanted. Safety, tenderness and laughter with a wonderful man who loved her and her children as much as all three of them loved him.

EPILOGUE

Cole straightened pillows on the new sectional sofa facing the window and stood back to appraise the room. After six months of planning and work, Kat and Dani claimed the space was decorated in just the way Alyssa would like best.

He liked the warm brown tones accented with aqua highlights and the contemporary feel, but his tastes didn't matter. This house was for Alyssa. He wanted her to have the house she'd said was her favorite house in Pacific Bay on their first day together.

Cole heard the front door open, and he hurried to the entrance to meet her. Awed by her appearance, he stopped short of greeting her.

Man she was something to look at. And he did, drinking in her sleeveless dress in a deep plum that hugged all of her curves and would make it hard for guests to keep their eye on Kat when she walked down the aisle today. Her hair was pulled up, and soft tendrils framed her face.

She looked up from dropping her keys into her purse and shivery earrings caught the light. "Cole? What are you doing here?"

"I wanted to surprise you."

"I don't understand." Her eyes narrowed and she studied him. "You're not dressed for the wedding so I'm guessing you're not here to drive me to the church after my showing."

"I'll change in a minute. My things are in the bedroom."

"Here?" Her voice shot up, and he couldn't stand not to tell her any longer.

"I bought this house a few months ago."

"You what?"

"You said this was your favorite house in town. I bought it and had my sisters furnish it."

He expected a radiant smile but got an even more confused look in return. "But I don't understand. You live and work in Portland. Why would you want a house here?"

Starting to wonder if he made the right decision, he took her hand and looked into her eyes. "After how I was able to work through my problems here at the beach, I thought it'd be nice to have a beach house in the family. You know, as a place for everyone to escape to when life gets too tough. And if I was going to buy a place, why not buy the house you love?"

"I see," she said. She still sounded disappointed and he hadn't a clue why.

He hadn't planned to take the next step until the reception tonight, but maybe now was the time to spring his other surprise. "Hold that thought," he said and ran down the hall to the master bedroom.

He dug in the dresser drawer and pulled out the ring box that had been sitting there since he'd closed on the house. He wanted everything to be perfect for his proposal, and he'd planned and coordinated it all with Kat to take place at her reception, but sometimes life throws a curveball and you have to act.

He only hoped Alyssa was more amenable to this surprise than she'd been to the house.

* * *

Alyssa went to the window and looked at the surf gently rolling in and tickling the feet of tourists. She loved living near the ocean, but after all her discussions with Cole in the past few months, she felt certain he was going to propose. She'd imagined she and the children would move to Portland to live with him. But the purchase of this house could mean she'd read his signals wrong and he thought they needed more time in their long-distance relationship to get to know each other.

She heard him come back into the room. "This house really does have the most incredible views."

"I agree. It's an amazing view," he said, his tone low and husky.

She turned and caught an appreciative look directed at her—not at the waves crashing on the shore. Her breath caught and for a moment she couldn't look away. He crossed toward her and her heart kicked into high gear, surprising her with the intensity of the beat. After two children and the loss of a husband, she hadn't thought she'd ever experience such a feeling again, but she loved Cole with everything she had.

He stopped in front of her and took her hand before going down on one knee. Shocked, her hand flew up to cover her open mouth and tears formed in her eyes.

He smiled up at her, his grin infectious. "I was planning to wait until the reception today, but you looked so unsure when I told you about the house that I thought I'd better ask now." Not taking his attention off her, he opened his hand. In the palm rested a black velvet ring box. He flipped it open. "Will you marry me, Alyssa, and make me the happiest man in the world?"

Tears rolled down her cheeks and she could barely speak, but she managed to squeak out a yes.

He slipped the ring on her finger, stood and wrapped his arms around her waist. "I'd also like to adopt Riley and Brianna, if you'll let me."

"Of course," she said, her heart overflowing with love.

"And then we can talk about giving them

a few more siblings. And we'll have that big family you've always dreamed of."

"I can't wait to tell them."

"Me, either, but I think we can hold off long enough for a kiss, don't you?"

Instead of answering, she cupped the back of his head and drew it down. Their lips met and he hauled her against his body, not a breath of air between them. She twined her arms around his neck and kissed him.

Cole's phone rang and with a groan, he pulled back but kept one arm around her lower back. "Sorry, but that could be Kat trying to find out where I am." He dug out his phone.

"I'm on my way, Kit Kat," he said in way of an answer.

As he listened, Alyssa trailed a finger near his ear. He swatted at her hand, but she continued her movements.

"Relax, Kat, I said I'm coming," Cole said and then hung up. He stowed his phone and grabbed Alyssa's finger. "You better stop that so I can get dressed, or you'll have to deal with bridezilla when we get to the church."

He laughed and she loved the sound of the deep rumble. He planted a chaste kiss on her forehead then headed down the hall.

Alyssa wandered the main floor of the home, running her finger over the smooth quartz countertop and admiring the furnishings. She couldn't have done a better job of decorating a house to her tastes if she'd done it herself. Memories of endless decorating discussions with Dani and Kat popped into her head. The sneaks had both claimed they were planning to do some redecorating and wanted Alyssa's input.

Cole returned, wearing a black tux and white shirt. The jacket was cut to emphasize his broad shoulders and toned body.

"Wow!" she said and searched for other words to add but couldn't find any. "Just wow."

Grinning in that playful lopsided manner that got her heart rate going, he headed her way. She knew he planned to kiss her again.

She held up a hand. "We have no time for a kiss. Remember bridezilla."

"Fine," he said and snagged her hand. "But be prepared for lots of kissing later."

They hurried to the car and held hands for the short drive to the church. Riley and Brianna stood on the steps with Dani, all of them part of the large wedding party. Behind them stood Ethan, Derrick and the groom, wearing tuxedos that matched Cole's. Ethan had his arm possessively around his wife, Jennie.

"Where have you been?" Dani eyed them with suspicion.

Alyssa held out her hand and Dani's gaze flew to Cole's. "I thought you were going to wait."

"Are you kidding? And give the single male wedding guests hope of a date with her?" Cole laughed.

The others congratulated them, and after the hubbub died down, Alyssa sat on a stone planter and took her children's hands.

Cole joined them and lowered himself to one knee by Brianna. She immediately climbed onto his knee and wrapped her arm around his neck to snuggle close to him. Riley, however, looked at them with suspicion.

She took a deep breath. "Remember how we talked about the fact that Cole and I love each other and that it was possible we could get married in the future?"

"Yeah," Riley said and Brianna nodded.

She held out her hand. "He asked me to marry him and I said yes."

Brianna squealed with delight and threw both arms around Cole. Riley stood like a soldier, casting a wary look at Cole.

"And," Cole said, settling Brianna back on his knee. "Though I can never replace your real dad, I want to make our relationship official and adopt you."

Riley's eyes widened. "Really? You mean it? Like we can play ball and stuff like Dad and I used to do?"

"Yep," Cole answered. "Just like that."

"Then I'm in." Riley held out his hand for a fist bump.

Cole connected then pulled Riley into his free arm and drew both of her children close. "Nothing could make me prouder than to be your dad."

Alyssa smiled over the twins at the man who would stand beside them in the good times and the bad. And just as Kat and Mitch would pledge their vows today, she knew this man would be next to her on life's journey no matter what came their way.

* * * * *

Dear Reader,

Thank you for reading Cole and Alyssa's story. The verse I chose for this book, Isaiah 26:3, comes from my own struggles in life. As I mentioned in my last book, I live with a chronic illness. On the days when pain is extreme, it's hard not to focus on the illness and let it take over my life. The problem seems big and overwhelming. I get down and struggle to overcome it.

But over the years of dealing with this issue in my life, I have learned that if I take a deep breath and turn my focus to God and on knowing that He has a plan for my life—including the pain and illness—I can overcome and find peace.

I hope that if you have problem areas in your own life, that Alyssa and Cole's story has helped you embrace Isaiah 26:3 and you can change your focus to find that perfect peace.

I love to hear from readers. You can reach me through the contact page on my Web site: www.susansleeman.com or in care of Love Inspired Books at 233 Broadway, Suite 1001, New York, NY 10279.

Susan Sleeman

Questions for Discussion

1. Cole blames himself for something he failed to do when in reality his friend's death was not his fault. Is there something in your life that you are blaming yourself for and need to let go? If so, how can you do it?

2. Alyssa has been hurt by two men that she trusted. We've all been hurt by those we love, but has anyone ever seriously betrayed you? If so, what can you take away from this story to help you heal from that betrayal?

3. Why do you think it took Cole so long to let go of his guilt over losing his friend?

4. After losing his friend, Cole turned away from God. He didn't restore his relationship for a few years. Has anything ever made you turn away? Maybe not for years but just for a day or so. What caused you to step away, and how could it have been different if you hadn't walked away?

5. At one point in the book, Alyssa thinks that God has brought her and Cole together so they can heal emotionally. Has God ever placed someone in your life for the purpose of healing?

6. When *No Way Out* opens, Cole hasn't worked through his survivor's guilt, but if he'd at least stopped focusing on the problem, his life could've been more peaceful. Is there a problem in your life that you're focusing on? Can you see how changing your focus to God and not dwelling on the problem will help?

7. When Alyssa's husband, Todd, died, her son, Riley, took on the responsibility of his sister. Have you ever assumed a responsibility like this, and, if so, how has it changed your life?

8. Alyssa is concerned that her children's loss of their father and Nolan, who'd stepped in as a father figure, will have a long-lasting impact on their lives. How have past hurts or events shaped your life?

9. Alyssa is faced with many obstacles in *No Way Out* that challenge her faith, but she always manages to hold on to it. Is there something in your life that is challenging your faith right now? If so, how can Alyssa's struggles help you with your own challenge?

10. *No Way Out* is book three in the Justice Agency series, and by now you have read about the dynamics of the five Justice siblings. Which of the brothers and sisters do you relate to most and why?

11. Dani Justice is a cheerful, easygoing woman who is successful in living her faith each and every day. Are you or do you know someone who has the same peace and tranquility all the time? If you aren't living like this, can you think of a way to change?

12. Cole is overprotective of everyone in his family but especially Dani because she is the baby in the family. If you have sib-

lings, where do you fall in the birth order and do you see the same family dynamics? How has that affected your life?

REQUEST YOUR FREE BOOKS!

2 FREE RIVETING INSPIRATIONAL NOVELS IN TRUE LARGE PRINT PLUS 2 FREE MYSTERY GIFTS

Love Inspired® SUSPENSE

TRUE LARGE PRINT

YES! Please send me 2 FREE Love Inspired® Suspense True Large Print novels and my 2 FREE mystery gifts (gifts are worth about $10). After receiving them, if I don't wish to receive any more books, I can return the shipping statement marked "cancel." If I don't cancel, I will receive 3 brand-new true large print novels every month and be billed just $7.99 per book in the U.S. or $9.99 per book in Canada. That's a savings of at least 33% off the cover price. It's quite a bargain! Shipping and handling is just 50¢ per book in the U.S. and 75¢ per book in Canada.* I understand that accepting the 2 free books and gifts places me under no obligation to buy anything. I can always return the shipment and cancel at any time. Even if I never buy another book, the two free books and gifts are mine to keep forever.

124/324 IDN FV2K

Name _____ (PLEASE PRINT) _____

Address _____ Apt. # _____

City _____ State/Prov. _____ Zip/Postal Code _____

Signature (if under 18, a parent or guardian must sign) _____

Mail to the Harlequin® Reader Service:
IN U.S.A.: P.O. Box 1867, Buffalo, NY 14240-1867
IN CANADA: P.O. Box 609, Fort Erie, Ontario L2A 5X3

* Terms and prices subject to change without notice. Prices do not include applicable taxes. Sales tax applicable in N.Y. Canadian residents will be charged applicable taxes. Offer not valid in Quebec. This offer is limited to one order per household. Not valid for current subscribers to Love Inspired Suspense True Large Print books. All orders subject to credit approval. Credit or debit balances in a customer's account(s) may be offset by any other outstanding balance owed by or to the customer. Please allow 4 to 6 weeks for delivery. Offer available while quantities last.

Your Privacy—The Harlequin® Reader Service is committed to protecting your privacy. Our Privacy Policy is available online at www.ReaderService.com or upon request from the Harlequin Reader Service.

We make a portion of our mailing list available to reputable third parties that offer products we believe may interest you. If you prefer that we not exchange your name with third parties, or if you wish to clarify or modify your communication preferences, please visit us at www.ReaderService.com/consumerschoice or write to us at Harlequin Reader Service Preference Service, P.O. Box 9062, Buffalo, NY 14269. Include your complete name and address.

REQUEST YOUR FREE BOOKS!

2 FREE INSPIRATIONAL NOVELS IN TRUE LARGE PRINT
PLUS 2 *FREE* MYSTERY GIFTS

Love Inspired
TRUE LARGE PRINT

YES! Please send me 2 FREE Love Inspired® True Large Print novels and my 2 FREE mystery gifts (gifts are worth about $10). After receiving them, if I don't wish to receive any more books, I can return the shipping statement marked "cancel." If I don't cancel, I will receive 3 brand-new true large print novels every month and be billed just $7.99 per book in the U.S. or $9.99 per book in Canada. That's a savings of at least 33% off the cover price. It's quite a bargain! Shipping and handling is just 50¢ per book in the U.S. and 75¢ per book in Canada.* I understand that accepting the 2 free books and gifts places me under no obligation to buy anything. I can always return the shipment and cancel at any time. Even if I never buy another book, the two free books and gifts are mine to keep forever.

117/307 IDN FVZK

Name _____ (PLEASE PRINT) _____

Address _____ Apt. # _____

City _____ State/Prov. _____ Zip/Postal Code _____

Signature (if under 18, a parent or guardian must sign)

Mail to the **Harlequin® Reader Service:**
IN U.S.A.: P.O. Box 1867, Buffalo, NY 14240-1867
IN CANADA: P.O. Box 609, Fort Erie, Ontario L2A 5X3

* Terms and prices subject to change without notice. Prices do not include applicable taxes. Sales tax applicable in N.Y. Canadian residents will be charged applicable taxes. Offer not valid in Quebec. This offer is limited to one order per household. Not valid for current subscribers to Love Inspired True Large Print books. All orders subject to credit approval. Credit or debit balances in a customer's account(s) may be offset by any other outstanding balance owed by or to the customer. Please allow 4 to 6 weeks for delivery. Offer available while quantities last.

Your Privacy—The Harlequin® Reader Service is committed to protecting your privacy. Our Privacy Policy is available online at www.ReaderService.com or upon request from the Harlequin Reader Service.

We make a portion of our mailing list available to reputable third parties that offer products we believe may interest you. If you prefer that we not exchange your name with third parties, or if you wish to clarify or modify your communication preferences, please visit us at www.ReaderService.com/consumerschoice or write to us at Harlequin Reader Service Preference Service, P.O. Box 9062, Buffalo, NY 14269. Include your complete name and address.

LITLP13TR

ReaderService.com

Manage your account online!

- Review your order history
- Manage your payments
- Update your address

*We've designed
the Harlequin® Reader Service
website just for you.*

Enjoy all the features!

- Reader excerpts from any series
- Respond to mailings and
  special monthly offers
- Discover new series available to you
- Browse the Bonus Bucks catalogue
- Share your feedback

Visit us at:

ReaderService.com

Initial Here
G -B- BB -JJ